Ser

Vol. IV

By Cassie Wild and M.S. Parker

Copyright © 2015 Belmonte Publishing
Published by Belmonte Publishing.

ISBN-13:
978-1514254622

ISBN-10:
151425462X

Table of Contents

Chapter 1

Aleena

"Dominic...it's Penelope. I just wanted to thank you for an amazing dinner."

The words connected, I guess.

They made sense, I guess.

But...

Shaking my head, I pulled away from Dominic and glanced toward the phone, then back to him.

It was the look on his face that did me in.

If I'd seen any *other* look on his face, I might have been able to curl back up against him and laugh it off, let things get back to where they'd been heading. I'd already had my fill of Penelope Rittenour and could already guess at the mindset

1

that woman had. She was the sort who'd just twist people up because she could.

But the look on his face, I couldn't ignore it.

His jaw was like stone and his eyes were icy, a cold glacial blue when he looked at me. Without a word, he rose and walked over to the counter. He deleted the message and then turned back towards me. When he sat down, I turned so that I was facing him, but not touching him.

"I thought you were having dinner with your mother," I said, trying to keep the accusation from my voice.

"She'd invited Penelope." He sat down and reached for me.

I didn't want to hear anymore. I stood up, but didn't make it three steps before he caught my wrist.

"Lovely," I said, giving him the smile I'd perfected for the business meetings I'd attended with him. It was all professional polish with zero emotion. "I imagine the two of them had a wonderful time telling you how absolutely *exotic* and *low-class* I am."

"I don't give a damn what they think about you!" His voice was harsh, the words boomed out in sharp staccato.

"Neither do I!" I fired back at him. Except I lied. When you've lived most of your life being the town freak because your skin's too dark for one group and too light for another, you grow a thick skin. But still, under that thick skin were layers and layers of nerves longing for acceptance. I could bluster through this though. I knew it. I'd done it before. I sneered at him, hoping that if I provoked him, he'd get angry and let me go. "You think I care what some New York princess with a pedigree thinks about me?"

Dominic lifted a hand and touched my cheek. The gentleness of it caught me off guard. I'd been expecting anger following my attack.

And then he murmured, "Yes."

I jerked away from his hand, shaking my head. "No, I don't."

"You do," he insisted. "Not so much what *Penelope* thinks and that's good, because she's not worth it. She can barely hold a thought in her head that doesn't revolve around the current trends and the current causes."

I felt a burst of relief at his description of Penelope, but it didn't overshadow the rest of what I was feeling. He took a step toward me to close the ground I'd managed to gain. I took another step back and found myself up against one of the low, fat accent chairs. I braced my hands against it, curling my fingers into the leather cushions.

"No, what you care about is how some people look through you and they look around you and they look down...and it hurts." He cradled my face, his thumb stroking across my lip. "I see you, Aleena."

I set my jaw, trying to ignore the way his words twisted my heart.

"I'm sorry." He pressed a soft kiss to my brow. "I should have mentioned it, but it was something my mother set up and I didn't want to upset you. I..." He looked away and then back at me, sighing. "I upset you more by not telling you."

No shit.

I eased away from him and moved to stare outside. Needing air, I pushed open the curtains to the rarely used balcony and stepped outside. The wind was still bitter cold, especially this high up, but I welcomed it and lifted my face, breathing it in. The robe I was wearing was thick, warm cotton, keeping me from freezing.

"Are we trying to make a relationship work here, Dominic?" I asked when I felt him move out behind me.

"I thought we'd already decided we were."

I nodded. Then, slowly, I turned to face him. "Then don't do this again. I understand why you didn't tell me, but it felt like you were hiding it."

Chapter 2

Aleena

We'd spent most of the weekend acting like...well, a couple. We watched movies. We ate together. When Dominic was taking phone calls in his office, we lounged on the couch. I did some work, but not a lot.

It was probably the easiest couple of days we'd had together.

Then, early Monday rolled around.

The sun wasn't even a whisper on the horizon when Dominic knocked on my door.

We still didn't share a bed.

I wasn't entirely certain how I felt about that. Part of me was glad, but part of me felt that deliberate, thin line of separation almost too keenly. I was good enough to fuck, even to doze next to a bit, but not good enough to spend the night in his bed, even though mine was only a few feet away.

When he knocked, I got up, tired but

5

unconcerned.

It hadn't been the first time he'd woken me up early with some business emergency. A few times he'd been going out of town. Twice, I'd been expected to throw some things in a bag and join him. Fawna hadn't been kidding when she'd said I'd need to basically be on call twenty-four / seven.

Sleepy and knuckling my eyes open, I stood there, waiting for him to tell me what he needed.

When he held out a hand, I stared at it stupidly for a moment and then accepted. That had been forty minutes ago.

"That's not the answer I'm looking for, Aleena."

I blinked back tears and shuddered.

"You didn't trust me."

He brought the cat down on my bottom again and pleasurable pain streaked through me. I bit my lip but couldn't stop myself from moaning. A few months ago, if anybody had told me I'd not only *let* a man tie me up, but that I'd also stand there and let him whip me, I would have told them to see a doctor. Fast.

But here I was, my hands tied behind my back, my feet on the floor, back bent, my ass in the air, exposed. I was torn between twisting away before the next blow could come down and lifting myself up in anticipation. It was both pleasure and pain, more intense than anything I'd ever felt before.

He'd started out with the same cat o' nine tails he'd used just a few days ago. Then he'd told me he was very upset with me and that if I didn't apologize for not trusting him, then he'd punish me even more.

Now, face flushed with embarrassment and with heat and with excitement, I trembled on the edge of something huge.

His hand fisted in my hair as he bent over me and I felt the hand on the whip prodding me between my thighs.

"You're being very stubborn today, Aleena."

"I'm sorry, sir," I said it automatically. I wondered if it should scare me that I found submitting to him so easy, but it didn't. I didn't do it anywhere but here and like this.

Dominic cocked his eyebrow, a faint smile curling his lips. His bright blue eyes had darkened to the deep blue of late summer sky. "And why are you sorry?"

"For being stubborn."

He pushed the handle of the whip harder against me and abruptly, I realized it wasn't accidental. I cried out as it slid easily against my sensitized flesh, between my wet lips, against my clit.

"You should trust me, Aleena."

I swallowed, but said nothing. It hadn't been a question, so I knew better than to answer.

He straightened and I braced myself for the whipping to start again. I didn't know if I could take much more. My ass was already on fire, but at the same time, I *wanted* more. I didn't understand what this man did to me, only that he knew things about me that I'd never imagined about myself.

Dominic turned me around, then sat me on the bed.

I cried out at the brush of my stinging flesh rubbing against the cool, slick texture of the sheets. He had stripped the bed down, made it ready for us with black silk sheets. I flinched in pain, then shuddered in ecstasy. I couldn't tell just where on the line I rode just then, but I wanted more.

He held me upright, one hand cupped around my neck. It was surprisingly difficult to sit on silk sheets with my hands tied behind my back.

With his other hand, he slowly pulled down his zipper. "I've decided how I'm going to punish you, Aleena."

The low, rough sound of his voice had a quiver running through me and I squirmed miserably. I wasn't sure which was worse, the burn on the skin of my ass or the ache between my legs.

"You want to come?" he asked.

I nodded.

He freed himself and I watched, mesmerized as he wrapped his hand around his cock and started to stroke the thick shaft. I licked my lips.

He pressed the head of his cock to my mouth. "Open."

I remembered the taste and weight of it all too well. He didn't have to ask me twice. I parted my lips.

He fed me one slow inch, his hand steadying my head and making it clear who was going to control this. "I want you to suck on it." He made a sound when I complied. "Now...swirl your tongue..."

He instructed me on how to suck his cock, each word like liquid sex dripping on my skin. His hips rocked back and forth, going from slow and lazy to deep and hard.

I flinched as he pushed too far and he immediately pulled back. I looked up, expecting disappointment. Instead, I saw the last thing I expected. Patient concern. I nodded and was rewarded with a flash of pride.

"Take a deep breath," he said as he eased back inside. I didn't need him to tell me that he was going just as deep. "Now...swallow it."

My lungs burned and my throat constricted, the muscles spasming around the width of him. But I fought to keep him inside, fought my body saying it was too much. I focused on the way my lips were stretched painfully wide around his base, the ache in my jaw.

"That's it...that's it..." he crooned.

He pulled out and did it again and it was easier. He didn't try to move fast, knowing I wasn't ready for that. Then he wrapped one hand around the base of his dick and began to fuck my mouth, his hand stopping him from going too deep. I moaned, unconsciously moving with him, desperate for more friction, but knowing better than to touch myself unless given permission.

He abruptly pulled back and I tried to follow, but he held me away with his fist in my hair.

Dazed, I stared at him and watched as he pumped himself with hard, rapid strokes. He came and I stared, startled as it splashed on my breasts, my legs and his hand. I'd had sex, but I'd never actually watched a man come, not like that.

"That's your punishment, Aleena."

Semen clung to my breasts and I watched as Dominic picked up a towel that had been sitting on the edge of the bed. He wiped his hands, then my breasts and legs, his movements gentle, but not sexual. He untied my hands next and I rubbed my wrists.

"You don't get to come this time."

My jaw fell open and I glared at him. "You—"

He jerked me upright and I ended up pinned between him and one of the thick pillars of the four poster bed. "This is how a relationship with a Dom works, Aleena," he whispered, his voice a low growl against my ear. "You have to trust me. Always. You didn't."

Slowly, he lifted his head and stared down at me as if waiting for my response.

I pushed up onto my toes and stared at him. Hard. The sex was done apparently, and I was too worked up to worry about whether or not he was still supposed to be in charge.

"You didn't trust me either." I barely resisted the

urge to poke him in the chest.

He frowned and stepped back. I couldn't tell if he was surprised at what I'd said or that I'd said it at all. His voice was soft as he spoke, "I guess that's something we'll both have to work on." He didn't look at me as he walked out of the room.

***

I took my sweet time showering since it involved some good old-fashioned therapy with the massaging shower-head. It wasn't even close to the same, but at least I wouldn't be jumping out of my skin the next time he came near me.

Part of me was pissed off at him.

The other part of me was still trying to catch up with the crazy turns my life had been taking lately. I wanted him to dominate me, but there were times I still resisted, feeling like I wasn't quite as there for him as he was for me.

"Did you enjoy your shower?"

I yelped at the sound of his voice and spun around, glaring at him when I saw him standing outside my bedroom door. Swallowing, I lifted my chin. "What was that?"

With a faint smile, Dominic shoved off the wall and came to me, the slow, rolling walk of a predator.

"The shower, Aleena." He dipped his head. "I heard you moaning."

I flushed. Then I shrugged. "I told you that you could teach me all about submitting when we're in the bedroom, Dominic. Your bedroom." I glanced around pointedly. "This is mine." My private quarters, I wanted to add, but I didn't.

It wasn't so much that I minded him being here, but the fact that he'd just come in enhanced the feeling that he didn't see me as a person, but rather a possession he owned.

"True enough." He held out a hand.

I put mine in his. I didn't want to feel this way, but it was hard when he closed himself off so abruptly. He pushed up the arm of my robe and looked at my wrist.

"I should have put lotion on these." He raised my hand and pressed his lips against the inside of my wrist. "I'm sorry. I'm still getting used to the after part."

That mollified me a little. Not much though.

"You never answered me," he said. "About whether or not you enjoyed your shower."

"It got the job done." I scowled at him, hoping he'd get the very intentional double meaning.

I saw a glimpse of anger flash across his eyes and then it was gone. He took a step back and I knew the personal part of our discussion was over.

Shrugging it off, I thought about the agenda. "The morning is fairly light—"

He lifted a hand and I fell silent.

"If you don't mind, I have an interior decorator coming by. She's a friend. Her name is Annette. It's been a while since I've had my penthouse decorated and I'm ready for a change. I'll need you to deal with her. I've got a morning of phone calls to deal with."

I frowned. "You were supposed to be talking to Mr. Kim today."

"We're rescheduling until his translator is feeling better." He rubbed at his jaw. "They're looking to talk again later in the month."

"Okay." I picked up my phone from my dresser. "Did you have anything in mind for the decorator?"

"Annette knows what I like."

I tried not to read anything else into that, but I was picturing the couch in the living room and I wondered if his thoughts had gone where mine had. And then I wondered if his comment had meant that Annette had been bent over that same couch. I pushed it away and tried to focus.

"Understood," I said. "Is...ah...would you like me to get anything else done while you're in the office?"

He glanced back at me and then nodded. He made mention of a name I'd heard before and after a few seconds, I placed it. "Start digging up as much as you can on them. How much money they pull in, what their debt is, any notable clients."

I made a note on my phone, frowning absently as I did so. "This company—it's not local."

"No. It's a matchmaking company down in

Philadelphia. I've been thinking of branching out and there's a small company there, owned by a friend, Edward Hall. Eddie's been planning to retire in a few years and when he heard about *Trouver L'Amour,* he asked if I had plans to expand." Dominic shrugged and said, "I told him I wouldn't commit to anything until I had an idea on how things were going here, but if it went well I wouldn't object to expanding."

He flashed me a wide smile. "But I plan for things to go well and he knows it. So Eddie told me to keep him in mind, because he spent a long time building his company and he'd like to pass it on into good hands."

His smile faded and he now simply looked grim. "*Devoted* must have heard about him retiring because they're moving in on his clients, talking to other people. It looks like they're pressuring him to sell, staking their claim."

I waited.

Dominic smiled as he looked away. "I wasn't sure I'd want to branch out so soon, but I like Philadelphia."

"So you're going to force them to sell...to you."

"They started it," Dominic said lazily. "If they'd left Eddie alone, it wouldn't have been an issue, but now...?"

The smile on his face could only be described as predatory, and not in a good way.

I thought I was very, very glad I wouldn't ever

14

come up against him in business. I wouldn't last very long. Then I made a few notes on my phone and put it down. He glanced down as if suddenly realizing I was still in my robe. He quickly excused himself so I could dress.

By the time I'd finished and headed downstairs, Dominic was in the kitchen. "Francisco will be in today," I said. "Is there anything you'd like him to prepare for you this week?"

"Lasagna. For some time later this week, though. I'm in the mood for chicken tonight. I'd like it ready when I get home. I shouldn't be working late."

I mentally ran his schedule through my head and compared it to when Francisco normally left. "I'll talk to him."

He nodded and came behind me. When he pressed a quick kiss to the delicate skin behind my ear, I shivered. He left without a word.

I closed my eyes and braced my hands on the table.

Normally, I'd go into the office and get to work, but that would involve sitting *down* and that wasn't something I'd want to do much of. At least not for a little while.

***

I hadn't known what to expect from Annette Shale.

There were so many different people in Dominic's world—so many different women. Most of them came and went, but hardly anybody came to his penthouse. Actually, other than his mother and Fawna, *none* of them came to the penthouse.

It felt odd to step aside for the tall, vibrant redhead.

She was what I'd call exotic.

Vivid red hair—and unless her stylist was very talented, the hair was natural, because her eyebrows were the same shade. Her eyes were shamrock green. Her skin, by contrast, was only a few shades paler than mine.

Not altogether white bread there, I decided, although I couldn't really figure out just what I was seeing in her. Other than the fact that she was completely gorgeous.

When I smiled at her, she held out a hand and gave me an open, friendly smile and said, "Hello. You must be Aleena. Dominic's told me about you."

I shook her hand and stepped aside to let her in. She immediately came inside and tossed her coat and bag across one of the fat leather chairs and propped her hands on her hips.

"Please tell me he's going to let me do something other than the *Fashion Interior Flavor of the Month* this time." She glanced over at me.

"Ah..." I wasn't entirely sure what I was supposed to say to that.

Annette laughed and waved a hand. "Ignore me, honey," she said and I caught the hint of a southern drawl. Not a native New Yorker then, but a transplant like me. "I keep telling that man that he's allowed to put some personality in his home, but he just wants to go with what's *current*. I've told him a thousand times not to worry about trends. What do you *like*?" She shook her head in tolerant exasperation.

Damn.

I was going to like her.

Did I want to like her, though? I moved a little deeper into the room as I pondered that.

I wasn't sure. "Have you..." I tripped just the slightest over the words. "Worked with Dominic often?"

"Yes." She sighed. A faint smile curled her lips as she smoothed a hand down the back of the couch. "I ended up with him by accident, really."

"How did you accidentally end up working with Dominic Snow?"

She laughed again, the sound full and rich. A smile played on her full lips. "You ask that question like you know the man, Aleena."

"Well..." I took my time choosing my words. I didn't want to piss her off, nor did I want to say anything out of place. "Dominic is just a man who seems to know who and how he wants things done."

"Indeed he does," Annette agreed. She came around and sat down on the chair, crossing her long legs. She wore a beautiful suit of peacock blue, the colors complimenting her eyes and hair beautifully. She was able to lounge in the chair in that way some women had, like a queen reclining on a throne. She was graceful and gracious and classy.

And nice, dammit. If she wasn't so nice, I could have disliked her on principle alone.

"Dominic had hired my partner—*former* partner," she amended. "At the time, my former partner was also my husband. He'd set out to the job and had already taken a sizable deposit from Dominic and then..." Annette paused, a faint laugh escaping her. It didn't sound like she was amused though. "I came home one day and found that he'd emptied his closet. I wasn't a fool, so I checked the bank accounts. He'd emptied those as well."

I tried not to stare at her because I knew she'd think I was either pitying or criticizing her. I wasn't doing either. I was actually trying to figure out how in the world any man would want to leave someone like her.

She continued with a cynical edge to her voice, "And I have to be honest. I realized I'd been a fool to trust him. I found out he'd been embezzling from the company the two of us had built from the ground up. It was almost bankrupt and I didn't know what I was going to do. Many of the clients were threatening to sue me, press charges..." Her mouth tightened, then

18

softened. "Dominic came by the office to check on something when I was on the phone with my lawyer. I was on the verge of tears and he heard me. Most people would have left. Not him. He brought me a bottle of water and he sat there and he listened. Then he put me on a retainer."

"Wow."

"Yeah." The smile on her face was sad now. The smile of a woman who'd learned a hard, ugly lesson and come out wiser for it. "He told me to fire my attorney and had me talking to one of his. Within two weeks, nobody was growling at my door anymore and somehow, they'd tracked down that cockroach I'd married and the tramp he'd run off with. Dominic had me finish the job my husband had been hired to do and he was happy with it, so he hired me to head the team that did the interior design for all of Winter Corporations businesses." She looked towards one of the windows, a distant expression on her face.

I thought of the man who'd left not that long ago.

The man who tried to tell me he didn't handle emotion and caring well.

The man who'd tried to pay my asshole ex-manager just so I wouldn't get fired.

"That...sounds like Dominic," I said after a moment.

Annette simply nodded.

Annette left near four o'clock with a stack of ideas for everything from the living room to the guest room. She said she'd want to talk to Dominic about redoing the house in the Hamptons once she was done with the penthouse. I made a note of it and silently wondered if that meant she'd be doing my place too. I'd have to ask Dominic about that.

Francisco left not long after, leaving chicken in the oven. It would take an hour to finish baking, just in time for Dominic to get home.

Once they were gone, I found myself pacing the living room feeling out of place and stressed. As much as I hated it, I knew why.

Without realizing I'd walked down the hall, I stood in the door of what I was coming to think of as *the* room. My skin heated whenever I thought of it. The bed, with its four posters jutting up into the air, framed against walls of stark white. The hooks, prominently displayed against the wood.

Annette had paused in the doorway when we'd done a walkthrough of the penthouse and she'd just glanced at me, given me a quiet look, but said nothing. I didn't know if she could see anything on my face, but I knew what I'd seen on hers.

That room didn't confuse her the way it had me the first time I'd seen it.

And that left me wondering. Did she *know* about Dominic? And if she did, was it because she'd guessed...or for other reasons?

The thought of her *knowing* made me feel kind of miserable inside.

I found my hand going to my grandmother's necklace, wondering what she would have told me to do about the lump in my stomach. Then I flushed at the thought of my grandmother knowing about that room. I let go of my necklace and decided that it was time to get some work done. I would do my job and pretend that my insides weren't twisting into knots.

I tried, but I didn't do a very good job.

Chapter 3

Dominic

Considering I'd spent most of my day reliving a specific morning encounter, I left work feeling fairly accomplished.

I had a number of meetings set up in the near future, including a couple in Philadelphia. Dumb fucks shouldn't have tried to come play in my pool without talking with me first.

I'd also cleared away a number of other matters and had a teleconference with the board addressing some upcoming issues with the line of hotels and a few other big issues. There was nothing urgent, but Amber and I had worked almost seven hours straight without a break. Lunch had consisted of sandwiches at our desk and if she'd noticed my occasional lack of focus, she was too professional to say. Or she was just used to it by now. Most people who worked closely with me knew how I worked, even if they didn't realize why.

Some of my mind had been on work.

Everything else had been back at the penthouse and now I was planning on all the things I wanted to do to Aleena. *With* Aleena.

For Aleena.

I felt a stab of guilt as I remembered how I'd left her. I didn't regret denying her release. That was part of learning how to be a Submissive. No, I regretted that I hadn't soothed her wrists and made sure she understood that I wasn't trying to be cruel, but rather build the trust we needed between us for this to work.

When I unlocked the door, the scent of dinner hit me and my stomach growled, grumbling in protest to let me know that the sandwich I'd given it for lunch hadn't done much good.

I looked around for Aleena. We could eat...first. It would be wise, considering the evening I had planned. We'd both need our energy.

She wasn't there.

My stomach made another gurgling yowl and I went into the kitchen and found a covered plate waited on the table for me. I tugged over the warming cover, smiling as I uncovered roasted potatoes, asparagus and chicken. It was still steaming and when I cut into it with a fork, it fell apart.

Taking the plate with me, I headed for my office. If she was working, then she could just stop and join me. She would often get so focused on things, she'd lose track of time. I wondered if she'd even eaten lunch today. I frowned. I hoped she had. I didn't want her skipping meals.

That made me pause. Looking for her to join me for dinner wasn't strange. Sometimes Fawna and I would share a meal while we watched TV or went over plans for what was ahead in the week, but the place my mind had gone had been concern over her well-being. That was something new. That was 'taking care of' territory.

I was thinking about Aleena in ways that I'd never thought about anyone else. Suddenly, everything I'd been thinking about all day came flooding in all at once.

The plans I had for the night weren't the only things I was thinking of.

I was thinking about...us. Personal things. Intimate things.

I needed to slow down, but images came cropping up, all the things I wanted to do to her, with her, for her...fuck it.

I could deal with the worries and everything else later.

I shoved another bite of food into my mouth, impatience gnawing at me now.

The office was empty, so Aleena wasn't working. She wasn't in the small personal gym I had set up in the penthouse either.

No. She was in her apartment. And the door was

shut.

I could hear the low, muted noise coming from the TV. When I knocked, the noise was silenced and, a moment later, she opened the door. I stood there with my half-eaten dinner in one hand and felt like an idiot. She waited with her head cocked and a curious look on her face, like she couldn't imagine why I was standing there.

All day, I'd been half-imagining coming home to find her naked, or even half-naked on the couch, eagerly waiting for me to return. As desperate for me as I was for her.

Instead, she was wearing a pair of yoga pants and a too-big zipped-up sweatshirt that slipped down on one shoulder. She looked adorable, like she was settling in for a night. Alone.

That was what pissed me off. She was settling in for a night alone and all I'd been thinking about was us spending the night together.

As I stood there, the top slid further down her shoulder and the skin bared made my mouth water. My hands itched and I almost reached up to tug it back into place.

I didn't though.

The pale, faded green looked like it had been through many washings and she caught the material, pulled it bag into place absently, the gesture one of long habit. I wondered if it had always been hers or if she'd gotten it from some guy. A guy she wanted to remember...

"Is everything okay?" She glanced at my food and then up to me. "Is there something wrong with your dinner?"

"Um..." I frowned and then shrugged. "No, it's good. Did you get any?"

"Me? Oh. No. That was for you. I ordered Chinese in a while ago." A smile danced across her lips. "Kung Pao chicken."

The sweatshirt slid down again, tempting me.

I wanted to grab it and yank it off. Pull down that zipper until I could see what I suspected from her bare shoulder; that she wasn't wearing a bra underneath.

I wanted her naked.

I wanted her naked and downstairs and clearly thinking about the hours that had transpired between us and not about damn Kung Pao anything.

She looked...bored.

She didn't look at all like she'd been thinking about anything that had happened between us. Like it hadn't been haunting her every thought all day, making work nearly impossible.

That pissed me off, but I refused to let it show. I couldn't let her know how much I needed her, not when it was clear I wasn't affecting her the same way. I cut into another bite of chicken, staring at her as I slid the fork into my mouth. I took my time chewing, watching her the entire time, trying to decide what to do next.

She didn't squirm. A few weeks ago, maybe even

just a few days ago, she would have squirmed, been uncomfortable by the way I stared at her and by the drawn-out silence.

But not now.

She just stood there and waited.

"How did the meeting with Annette go?" I knew Annette would never have treated Aleena poorly, but I was curious as to how the two of them had gotten along. Next to Fawna, Annette was one of the few women I didn't always feel the need to keep up my guard.

"Oh, fine." Aleena shrugged, glancing back at the muted TV, as though her brain was already back on whatever program she wasn't watching. "She seems eager to get to work. She said she wants to do the house in the Hamptons too if it's all right with you. We'd need to go out there. If you can spare me any this week, I'll contact her and let her know when it will work."

I waited.

She looked back at the TV. Then back at me, her face still calm.

"Okay."

She smiled. "Okay, then." She looked at the plate. "I'll be sure to let Francisco know you enjoyed the meal."

"Ah, yeah. Please do." I looked down, realized I'd eaten almost seventy-five percent of it and for all I knew, it had been pure cyanide. "It was fine."

"Great." She smiled at me. A perfectly nice

smile. "I'll let you get back to your evening then."

She patted me on the shoulder and without really understanding how she did it, she managed to nudge me from the doorway and back into the hall. She closed the door and I stood there for a full minute, holding my plate and staring.

I almost drove my fist into the door, almost demanded she open up and let me in. I had a key if she'd locked it. I could just go inside, insist that she come with me, tell her that it was an order...

No.

I couldn't do that.

What I couldn't figure out was just how in the fuck had I ended up on the *outside* of her door when I'd planned on having her downstairs, tied up to the bed, begging for my cock?

***

Relationships.

I lay on my bed two hours later, staring out through the window and trying to figure out what had happened. And trying to ignore the part of my body that was highly annoyed that things hadn't gone the way I'd planned.

Something had to have happened, but I couldn't figure it out and it was pissing me off.

The longer it eluded me, the more frustrated I became and finally, I kicked my legs over the edge of the bed and grabbed my phone. I had to search through my contacts before I found Annette's number, but finally, I dug it up and put in a call to her.

I got her voicemail.

No, I didn't want to leave a message.

Pissed off was turning into angry.

I called Fawna next. I knew her number by heart and she huffed out a faint breath when I told her what I wanted. "Aleena has that information, you know, Dominic," she told me. In the background, I heard the fussy cry of a baby and I reached up, pinching the bridge of my nose, instantly feeling guilty.

"I'm sorry. I didn't wake him up, did I?"

She gave a tired laugh. "No. That would imply he'd been sleeping and he hasn't been doing much of that."

The ragged edge of the nerves in her voice would have gone unnoticed to someone else. But I wasn't someone else. Fawna was more my family than the parents who'd adopted me. "What's wrong? Eli's not sick, is he?" I lowered my hand, concern growing inside me. Concern and self-loathing. Here I was, moping over Aleena, and Fawna was dealing with a sick baby.

"No." She sighed and this time, when the baby made a noise, it was a weaker, soft sort of snuffle.

"He's not sick. He's just not doing well on his formula. I took him to the doctor today and we've got to start him on one for babies with sensitive stomachs. They told me to expect it, what with the drugs his mom had done and all the other health problems. I'd just hoped..." Her voice trailed off and then after a moment, she said, "The pediatrician gave me a recommendation for a new formula. I've got a few samples of it and he's already calmer. I'll give it a few days just to be sure before I buy any though. No use wasting money." Her tone shifted into business mode. "Now...give me a minute. I'll find Annette's number and you'll tell me why Aleena can't give you the information."

I grimaced and dropped back on the bed.

I should have just left it alone. I knew I didn't have a choice now though. Fawna wasn't going to leave it be.

A few minutes later, I had the number and I'd explained, sort of, to Fawna what had happened with Aleena.

"Has it occurred to you that maybe she just wanted a night alone?"

Scowling, I stared out the window at the night-darkened sky of New York City. Well, it was possible. But...I shook my head. Then, remembering Fawna couldn't see me, I said, "Something was just off. I can't think of what it was, but there was this distance between us."

"So why didn't you ask her?"

"What in the hell am I supposed to say?" I demanded.

"How about you ask her what's wrong?" Fawna suggested, an exasperated sound to her words that I recognized well from when she'd been my teacher rather than my assistant.

When I didn't respond, she cursed under her breath. Rubbing my neck, I closed my eyes. I was really starting to regret having called her.

"Dominic, you're a grown man and you're in a serious relationship—"

"No, I'm not."

I cut her off, the panic in my voice coming through loud and clear to both of us. My heart gave a nervous thud. There was silence for several seconds and I was suddenly having a hard time breathing.

"Aren't you?" Fawna finally asked.

Fuck. I squeezed my eyes closed.

"Dammit, Dominic!" she half-shouted through the phone. I had a feeling if Eli hadn't been there, she would've been louder.

I held it away from my ear as I turned away from the window. "Look, Fawna..."

"No. You look." Her voice was sharp, that no-nonsense voice that had given her command of the rowdiest students in the school. "You're a grown man, dammit. I realize that what happened messed you up. I know that. I understand and I'm sorry for it. But that doesn't mean you get to keep using it as an excuse. You're involved with Aleena. For fuck's

32

sake, you're sleeping with her! Now, are you or are you not serious?"

I closed my eyes. "I...I don't know, Fawna. I don't..." I passed the back of my hand over my mouth. "I don't know if I'm even ready to *think* about that."

"Maybe you should have considered that when you told me she was *good* for you." Fawna's voice was waspish and I knew it wasn't just lack of sleep. "Or did you mean she was good for your dick?"

She hung up.

It took me a few seconds to realize what she'd done and in a dull, dazed shock, I lowered the phone and stared at it.

She actually hung up on me.

I should be mad.

I might be later, but just then, I was too busy realizing something.

Fawna was right.

I'd only been thinking about one specific thing— or rather, one specific area—when it came to Aleena. We were good sexually. Scowling, I thought about all the clients I had coming and going through *Trouver L'Amour*. I didn't have much to do with any of them, not once I got them through the door. That was the matchmaker's job, not mine. I poured funds into the place and yeah, I'd been roped into working with Penelope, but the truth was, I was quietly talking to one of the top-level matchmakers I'd hired away from another company to take her off my hands.

There was a skill to this, an art almost. It was fun, in a way, I had to admit, seeing some of the people I knew get matched up, but I didn't believe in it. Not for myself. Even now. Not even with a woman like Aleena who made my brain go a little fuzzy and my heart rev up and race. We could have a relationship, but it couldn't be one with a real future.

Happy ever after was fine for others. Just not for me.

Still...I had to make myself admit something painful. Sooner or later, Aleena would want that. And she deserved it. I just didn't know if it meant I would have to give her up.

Or if I could.

Chapter 4

Aleena

"Girl, I gotta tell you, that look on your face? It's not the look of a woman who is well satisfied with her man."

I stared stupidly at Molly over the top of my menu. "My man?"

Molly stabbed a fork in my direction. "I *knew* it! Trouble in paradise!"

"What? No!" I brushed it off and flipped through the menu. I didn't want to talk about work or about Dominic. "I think I'm just going to get a Cubano and some sangria. What are you getting?"

"Some pliers and a dentist's drill, so I can get a straight answer out of you, no matter what it takes." Molly pulled the menu out of my hand and snapped it down on the surface of the table. Then she leaned forward. "Come on, Aleena. What gives?"

I absently picked up the little plastic encased

menu with the specials. Being purposely evasive, I said, "Nothing. Why you asking?"

"Because, one, you won't look at me and, two, you're drinking in the middle of the day. Dead giveaway." Her dark eyes narrowed. "Now, come on. I've a class in two hours."

"How is school going?" I latched onto a new topic with desperation. Molly had decided she wanted to go back to school recently and, normally, that was one thing guaranteed to distract her.

Not this time.

"Now, Aleena," she said ominously and leaned forward.

I sighed. I knew that look. I doubted she'd even be swayed if some hot stranger walked by, and that was saying something. So, I started to talk, feeling more and more like an idiot as I laid it out. I had to stop barely two minutes in as the server came by and took our orders. This was definitely not something I wanted anyone else to hear. I took the moment to enjoy the warmer air coming in through the windows. They were only open a bit, but it was enough to feel the promise of spring. I was so ready for it. Of course, I'd already lived through my first New York summer and I knew, in no time, I'd be ready for cooler temperatures again.

After the server left, I looked back at Molly.

"I'm starting to feel...out of place," I finally said.

"You don't even know if he has, or even had, anything going with this Annette woman." Molly caught my hand and squeezed it. "It sounds to me like he's pretty into you. And Penelope..." she made a face "...forget her. She's clearly on a power trip." Her eyes widened. "Shit, please tell me she's not that Penelope Rittenour—"

I shot her a look.

Molly's eyes widened even more. "Oh, shit. She is, isn't she?"

"How do you...?"

Molly grimaced. Then she dug into her purse, pulling out her phone. "Gimme a second."

A minute later, she handed me her phone. It had an article from ECHELON pulled up. It was one of the local New York society mags. One all about the rich, the powerful, and of course, the beautiful. I knew the name because I'd seen the interview he'd done for them when *Trouver L'Amour* had opened. I'd gotten the feeling he'd been annoyed by the whole ordeal and had only done it because he needed the promotion.

And now, Penelope Rittenour was on the front of the magazine.

The headline read: *Inside the Rittenour Experience*

I stared at it for a long moment and then looked at Molly. "Inside the Rittenour Experience?" I repeated it back to her.

Molly gazed back at me, her expression unreadable.

I had to bite the inside of my cheek to keep from

laughing. After a moment, I had it under control. "Okay, just *what* is the Rittenour experience? The life of a rich, privileged white chick?"

"Pretty much." Molly grinned at me.

The server appeared with our drinks and I was surprised to realize less than ten minutes had passed since I started detailing how crappy I'd been feeling over my so-called relationship with Dominic. The server gave us a basket of tortilla chips and salsa, and then lingered to smile at Molly. She smiled back, of course, but it was a distracted smile. She was clearly more focused on me and the Rittenour experience.

"You should read it." She scooped up some salsa with one hand and gestured with the other. "It's...riveting. She talks about the beleaguered life she's lived, being the only Rittenour left to carry on the family name and the weight of sustaining a life of social privilege and how hard it is to maintain grace and class in such a classless society. How nobody appreciates art and beauty anymore. She has a master's in fine arts and excelled in literature, yet when she attempted to publish a book about her family's legacy, there was no interest in it." Molly managed to deliver all of this with a downtrodden air and then she winked at me. "People would rather read about Snookie or sex or scandals instead of those who strive to better the lives of the rest of us poor folk."

I clicked on the image and skimmed through the

article, sipping from my sangria. "Poor thing," I murmured and passed the phone back to Molly before I dripped sarcasm on it.

"Please tell me you're not feeling outclassed by *her*."

I made a face. "No. She's an uptight bitch. And, FYI, she probably feels everything that's written in that article is one hundred percent true and that's she's been seriously put upon. The publishing world should have wept tears of joy when she gave them her masterpiece."

I snorted and took a healthy swig of my sangria then put it down. Brooding into its ruby red contents, I shrugged. "She isn't the problem. I've seen the way Dominic looks when I tell him he has a call from her. I don't like her, and it's clear he's not interested in her."

"If that's the kind of woman he wanted around him, I doubt you'd be able to stand working for him anyway. I was annoyed just reading it."

"How did you come across it?" Puzzled, I flicked a look up at her.

Molly snorted and sipped at her water. "Assignment for my Introduction to Sociology class. We were told to find examples of privilege in New York." She grimaced. "We're acting them out. We can't use names or anything, of course. I'm using her. She's kinda priceless."

I had another word for Penelope, but I decided not to name it.

"It's not her. It's the other woman then. The interior decorator." Molly leaned back as the server arrived to put our dishes down in front of us. We lapsed into silence until she was gone.

"It's not..." Then I groaned. No point in lying.

"It is." She pointed at me with her fork before digging in. "*She* makes you feel nervous. You feel like she's the kind of woman Dominic would be into, huh?"

Self-conscious now, I shrugged and focused on the food in front of me. "She's gorgeous, Mol. She's confident and friendly and she knows more about his world than I do."

"Does Dominic seem to think you have to know about his world?"

I delayed my answer by taking a drink of my sangria. Then I looked up at her. "I don't know. There are times..." I cleared my throat. "There are times when I know he's covering or helping me out. He wouldn't have to do it with her. Everybody in his world is rich." I laughed bitterly. "And most of them are white. The few that aren't? They're from some distinguished black families that can trace their ancestry back to people like Booker T. Washington. They're not some poor mixed girl from the mid-west."

"That doesn't mean shit."

"It does to some."

Molly leaned forward, glaring at me. "It doesn't mean *shit*," she repeated. "If they care, it says more

40

about them than it does about you. You can't let their prejudices bring you down, Aleena."

She held my eyes for a long moment and I made myself nod. She settled back in her seat and I forced air into my tight lungs.

"Dominic," she said softly. "Does it matter to him?"

"I don't think it does." I took another sip of sangria then looked down at my barely touched food. "But I've never come right out and asked him."

"You need to talk to him about it."

"Yeah." I pasted a smile on my face. It was as fake as the palms the restaurant had stuck in pots around us, but it seemed to convince Molly.

"Talk to him," she said again.

I nodded.

"I came here on a date a few weeks ago." Molly smiled at me over the rim of her water. "They have this crazy thing on the weekends. Salsa dancing. It gets all hot and sexy. Maybe you should have Dominic bring you down here."

I almost choked. Me...salsa dancing. With Dominic. Oh yeah, that would happen. Heat rushed to my face as I thought it again. Dancing. With Dominic.

"We...um...we don't really go out on dates," I said, shrugging the idea off as quickly as it came.

I went to say something else, but the look on Molly's face froze the words before they came out. "What?" I asked. Automatically, I lifted a hand to my

41

mouth. "Do I have food in my teeth?"

"You two don't go out?" Molly stared at me. "At all?"

"Well. No." I shrugged and pulled a piece of ham off the Cubano, popping it into my mouth. "What's up?"

"Aleena, you two have been...well...*involved* for a while, and Dominic Snow is kind of known for taking women out on some pretty elaborate dates. So why in the hell hasn't he taken *you* out?"

***

It bothered me.

As I worked all that afternoon and all that evening, I told myself I wasn't working to distract myself from that question. I was a liar.

It bothered me.

Why hadn't he taken me out?

I found myself constantly thinking about what Molly had said. Dominic had said he didn't do relationships, but I knew Molly wouldn't lie about him having taken women out on elaborate dates. She'd always loved gossip, especially about the New York elite. So, in the middle of researching the ritzy and very stable firm of *Devoted*...what happened?

I found myself googling Dominic.

Okay, it hadn't started *out* that way.

I started out googling the owner of *Devoted*.

The CEO was Maxine Hall and, while the company itself was stable, it became clear pretty fast that she wasn't. I spent more than a little time on her and found enough information that I figured Dominic would have something to play with. I was sure he had all sorts of investigators he could go to for more detailed information so I didn't bother trying to do that. I was good with computers, but I wasn't even close to a hacker.

But once I'd finished with what I could find, I found myself staring at the empty search bar.

And then...

Dominic Snow...

And I completely blamed Google, because the next thing that popped up was a single word: girlfriend.

Closing my eyes, I hit *enter* and then just let it happen.

I never should have done it, either.

I should have closed the damn browser and sent him off an email or even called him with my thoughts about *Devoted*. Jotted them down. Something. Anything but what I'd done.

After a few seconds, I gathered my courage and opened my eyes.

My gut twisted and bile churned.

Why in the hell hasn't he taken you out?

Molly's words echoed in my head.

I found myself staring at some sort of publicity

still, definitely a posed image. They were standing on a red carpet and he was in a tuxedo while the woman at his side wore a dress of champagne colored silk. It highlighted her eyes and set off her porcelain skin to perfection. Her eyes were a pale, soft blue.

She was absolutely beautiful.

Much of the world thought so too. *I* thought so.

That was Madeleine Bateman. I didn't need to read the caption to know who she was. She'd appeared in two of my favorite movies last year, and she'd appeared in no less than three images with Dominic last year too.

Before her? A woman who'd won two gold medals in the in Winter Olympics. A Russian ice skater, I thought. There was also a violinist from the New York Orchestra. A bestselling children's author. A biologist.

"Well," I said, trying to cheer myself up. "At least he seems to appreciate brains in a woman. That means Penelope is out of the running." Even hearing the words out-loud didn't really do much to perk up my mood.

I closed the window and then, because I felt like a fool, I cleared the search from my history and rose from the chair to pace.

I stopped by the window and stared down into the park, nibbling on my thumbnail until I realized what I was doing. It was a habit I'd broken in high school and there I was doing it again.

He was going to drive me crazy, I knew it.

Why in the hell hasn't he taken you out?

"It doesn't matter," I told myself.

I was getting really, really good at lying to myself.

Chapter 5

Dominic

"Mr. Snow?"

I glanced away from the information on *Devoted* that I'd gotten from one of my more trusted private investigators. I'd been about to call Aleena and see what she'd found out, although it wasn't anything that couldn't wait. I just wanted to talk to her. Sighing, I reached up and tugged at the knot on my tie before I answered, "Yes, Amber?"

"I've got Mr. White on the phone. He wants to talk to you about the party in Philadelphia?"

"Okay. I'll take the call." I went to pick up the handset, but Amber's voice made me pause.

"Ah, one moment, before you speak to him. I'll be—"

"This is nonsense, I'm sure Dominic won't mind if I wait in his office," a cool, crisp voice said, cutting Amber off.

I walked over to the door before I had to hear Amber trying to figure out how to stop Penelope from barging in. I opened the door just as Penelope was reaching for it.

"It's all right, Amber. Can you please let Eddie know I just need a moment?"

"Of course." She gave me a polite nod and didn't look at Penelope.

"Really!" Once the door closed behind her, Penelope spun to glare at me. "You should *fire* that woman, Dominic! She—"

"She did her job, Penelope," I said flatly. Her habit of barging in on me whenever she pleased was starting to go beyond annoying. "I don't have the kind of career where people can waltz in and out of my office as they please. I'm often involved in high-dollar, confidential matters that can fall apart in an instant. Amber clearly understands that."

I left the rest of the statement unsaid.

Penelope drew in a breath through her nostrils. Apparently, she didn't need me to spell things out for her. "Well, I simply wanted to touch base on how the matter was going with my...consult." She touched her tongue to her lip in what I suppose she assumed was a coy manner.

It wasn't.

Deliberately, I glanced at my phone to make it clear that I didn't have time for her. "That's a matter that would have to be discussed during a scheduled appointment. In order to give our clients our best, we do need to schedule time into the calendar for any meetings."

Harsh flags of color appeared on her cheeks. Her eyebrows rose over her hazel eyes and I knew I was treading dangerous waters, as far as Penelope's *consideration* went. Frankly, I didn't give a damn. Enough people in our social circle knew the type of person she was. I doubted she could do much damage on her own.

"Then when I can make an appointment?"

She gave me a tight smile as I came around the table and took her elbow. She allowed it, but her entire body was stiff, rigid. I was sure no one had ever dared to handle her with anything but kid gloves.

"Why don't you talk to Amber about scheduling an appointment?" I felt bad pawning Penelope off on Amber, but I wasn't in the mood today.

A few minutes later, Amber had her revenge and I had Penelope blocked out for my lunch hour today.

So much for having a few hours to myself.

At least I'd had the needed time to talk to with Eddie and see what was going on down in Philadelphia.

***

"Tell me about the party in Philadelphia."

49

From across the table, I met Penelope's eyes and wondered what it would take for her to leave me the hell alone. I had a feeling it would be a lot. She had her eyes firmly fixed on my net worth and the Snow name. She might already be imagining whether or not to hyphenate her last name.

Under the table, I curled a hand into a fist, one so tight it made my hand hurt.

"The one that doesn't concern you?" I answered curtly as I reached for the water glass.

A sommelier appeared with a wine list and I shook my head, starting to wave him away.

"Oh, come now, Dominic." She laughed softly and reached for it.

"Have what you want," I said, pulling my phone from my pocket and checking it. "Business expense and all." There were several emails from Aleena and my heart skipped just seeing her name. I couldn't take the time to read them here and I found myself growing even more impatient with my working lunch. "I'm due back at work shortly."

She made a low sound of dismissal. "One glass won't affect you, I'm sure. We'll try the '86 Mou—"

"The lady may have anything she wishes," I interrupted, staring hard at Penelope for a moment before looking up at the wine steward. I smiled at the young woman. It wasn't her fault Penelope thought she could lead people around by the fucking nose. "But I'll stick with water, thank you."

"Of course, Mr. Snow." She gave us both a polite

smile and looked back at Penelope and correctly guessed what Penelope had planned to order.

"Yes, that would be it." A dark frown marred her brow but for only a moment. It smoothed away in seconds. Too bad. Those few seconds of frowning gave her face more character than I typically expected from her.

As the server walked away, Penelope said coolly, "I apologize, Dominic. I simply thought you'd enjoy relaxing with a friend over lunch. How was I to know that a simple glass of wine would make you so uncomfortable?"

"Uncomfortable?" I laughed and the humorless sound made Penelope shift in her seat. Leaning forward, I said, "I'm hardly uncomfortable, Penelope. But this isn't the first time you've attempted to make a decision for me." I paused and let those words sink in. "I don't care for it."

"Ah..." She smiled and settled back in her chair. "Yes. You prefer your quiet, docile little toys like, what's her name? Adriana?"

"Her name is Aleena and you know it," I said calmly, refusing to rise to the bait. "I'll assume my mother told you that Aleena and I are involved."

"Sexually." Penelope made dismissive motion with one hand, a ring of platinum, rubies and diamonds flashing in the dim light. "It's not really surprising. A girl like that can only hope to rise above her station by using sex."

This time, when I laughed, I really was amused.

51

Aleena...using sex to get what she wanted. It was ridiculous. I was...

Now my laughter faded, because I had to admit the truth.

I was the one using her, if anything. Using her, because sex was all I'd ever allow myself, even if I did care for her. And I did.

My tone became serious. "Aleena doesn't use people." I fell silent as the sommelier reappeared, bringing Penelope's wine. I remained silent as she opened the bottle and it occurred to me how inane this whole thing was. Stupid, really. Although the wine steward made a lovely presentation of it, presenting the cork and the glass to Penelope, the bitch didn't bother to take the time to appreciate the wine or the time the sommelier had taken with the process, tossing back nearly a third of the wine like a sailor coming on shore leave.

I looked up at the sommelier and smiled. "Thank you."

She nodded and left as Penelope stared at me over the rim of the glass.

"Everybody uses people, Dominic. That's how the world works."

"For people in our world? Typically," I agreed then shrugged. Placing the phone on the table, I stroked one finger across the smooth glass surface and then said softly, "Yes, that is how our world works, but Aleena isn't from our world, is she?"

Penelope took another sip of her wine and then

put the glass down. "I didn't come here to discuss your...assistant."

She smirked as she said it and the expression in her eyes clearly relayed another message, but I just stared at her and waited. I knew better than to say something and let Penelope twist it.

"Have you had any luck finding a match for me?"

"There are a few." I named one.

"No." She curled her lip. "He's made noises recently about going into politics. I don't want to be a politician's wife."

I hadn't heard that. Interesting. The politics part, not what Penelope wanted. I was sure the life of a politician wouldn't appeal to her. Too much struggle to stay in the limelight without a scandal. "Travis Masters—"

"No. He's divorced and has a child. I don't want some other woman and a brat to compete with." Her eyes glinted over the rim of her glass.

Over the next twenty minutes, as we placed our orders and was served, I tossed out a few names—most of them random acquaintances—and Penelope shot down every last one of them.

"Penelope, has it occurred to you that you might be rather difficult to match up if you're this...selective?" I finally asked with an exasperated sigh.

She pushed her food around her plate and smiled at me. I realized I hadn't seen her take more than two bites of the expensive lobster bisque or its accompanying salad.

"I actually have somebody in mind who'd be ideal...Dominic." She speared a small, plump tomato with her fork and slid it between her lips, her lashes lying low over her eyes.

The woman was about as subtle as...well, I couldn't think of something that was less subtle than her.

"Is that a fact?" I placed my napkin down on the table and signaled for the server. I was done with this.

"You can't tell me you haven't thought of it."

Shifting my eyes back to hers, I elevated a brow. She was going to be that direct, was she? At least she'd stopped pretending to be coy.

She reached out a hand and covered mine. "I was thinking, perhaps what we need to do is take a few days away, just the two of us. Get to know each other. I've got a soiree of sorts coming up in Philadelphia next month. Perhaps you could attend with me...?"

"My plate is rather full." I pulled my hand out from under hers and reached for my wallet as the server laid the bill down, tucked inside a discreet leather folder.

"Dominic—"

I looked over at her. "I'll be in Philadelphia off and on myself over the next few months. I can possibly help set you up with a date for your event if you're looking for companionship—"

She jerked up, moving so quickly she banged into the table.

"Do you really think that *I* need help finding a man to attend a function with me?" She glared down at me, her eyes glittering, color rushing into her face. "The very idea is *absurd*. The only reason I've even talked to you about your *stupid* matchmaking company is because you're too obtuse to see what I'm offering you."

Rising to stand in front of her, I inclined my head. Penelope glared at me and all around us people were staring. I saw at least one with their phone out.

Leaning in, I said quietly, "Keep this up and you'll have some interesting commentary on social media to follow that piece ECHELON did on you."

Her mouth went tight but then, bit by bit, the tension faded and she smiled. The polite society mask was back in place. "Really, Dominic..."

That was all she said, and then she laughed. The odd, tense silence shattered and the pace around us resumed. I held out my arm and she took it. It didn't surprise me. It was the best thing to do to diffuse the scene.

As we stepped out in the brilliance of the spring day, a camera flashed in our faces. Penelope didn't even look fazed and I suspected I knew why. She'd contacted somebody, told them we'd be there. She hadn't planned on me turning her down, but she'd sure as hell set me up.

Now we'd end up on a local gossip site. Great.

It was nothing new to me, yet I was irritated all the same. Leading her to the curb where my car waited, I let Maxwell open the door for us, but after Penelope climbed in, I looked at him. "Take her wherever she wants. I'm walking back to the office. It's not far."

He gave me a nod. He'd been with my family my whole life and had often been more like a father to me than my adopted father had. He could tell with one look that I was annoyed and that Penelope was the cause.

Turning my back on the car, I pushed through the crowd of people and began to walk.

This whole mess was going to bite me on the ass, I knew it.

Penelope could cause trouble, and I knew that too. But I wasn't somebody she could jerk around, and that was something *she* needed to know.

My phone chimed and I pulled it out, reading the text from Amber. She had a firm date set in Philadelphia. In two weeks, I'd be meeting with White and the heads of *Devoted*. A nice, low-key— *bring your spouse and significant others...we're all friends here*—sort of event. I would attend, and then I'd cut them off at the knees and hand them their balls, financially speaking.

I had work to do.

Blowing out a breath, I wondered if maybe I

should have waited to piss Penelope off until after this event had passed. She would have made an excellent ice princess to have on my arm.

Although, really...Aleena could cut people off the knees rather well.

After all, she'd done a hell of a job on me.

58

Chapter 6

Aleena

Pacing never accomplished anything.

Except it burned off energy and it was better than chewing on my nails.

I'd paced until I'd all but worn a trail into the plush carpet and I didn't feel any better for it.

It was almost seven and I'd given up trying to work at least an hour ago.

I'd expected to be done well before now, but less than thirty minutes after my lunch with Molly, my phone had rung and it had been Amber on a conference call. Dominic had been the third person.

"We've got work to do," Dominic had announced and then he named a date. "That evening, Eddie White will be having a dinner party at his office location. It's for the VIPs at *Devoted* and other key personnel. The plan, they think, is for him to get them to lay off and let him work out until he's ready to retire. What is going to happen is that they are going to have their asses handed to them. Aleena, are you ready? I've got a list of names and I need you to dig up information on them. You should know what sort of information I need. I'll give you a couple names of some investigators you can trust to help out with some of the...less savory aspects."

That had taken up most of my day, and now he was due home. He'd want an update and I wanted to talk.

Could I convince him to go out for a drink? That would be...well, like a date, right? At least it would show he didn't mind being seen with me in public on something other than official business.

Before I could think the idea through and debate the merits of it, the door opened and I spun around, my head spinning from all the noise inside it. Dominic came striding inside and stopped abruptly, as though the sight of me standing there caught him off guard.

"Aleena."

My heart did a strange little dance, almost flipped around inside my chest at the sight of him, the sound of my name on his lips. "Dominic."

His eyes started to slide over me and heat danced along my spine. Then, abruptly, he looked away.

Cold replaced heat.

"Ah..."

"Did you get started on the information I needed?" he asked, his voice taking on that blunt, all-business tone I was so familiar with.

The one he hardly ever used with me anymore.

Slowly, I nodded, trying not to feel hurt. He was probably just concentrating on the deal. It was complicated.

Moving forward, I gestured toward the folders I'd organized on the low-lying coffee table. There were groups who'd have a field day with so much paperwork, but Dominic did better when he had hard copy in front of him. I made sure everything was recycled when he was done with it and we were careful to use recycled products as much as possible. Personally, I had too much data to deal with and did better when I could organize digitally, but one thing I'd learned quickly: everybody dealt with things better in their own way.

As he sat down and started to flip through my organized piles, I slid into the seat across from him.

He didn't even look at me.

There was no reason, really, for my heart to give a funny little lurch. Or the slightly sick feeling in my stomach when he kept his head down.

"Annette and I had to reschedule for the meeting out to the house," I said tentatively. "She...um...she's not feeling well. She wanted me to apologize."

"That's fine." He was clearly distracted, his gaze racing over the data I'd compiled for him. I'd already committed much of it to memory and I knew he was doing the same thing. It was strange that I'd found

61

myself working with somebody whose brain worked in a way not similar to mine, but complementary. "She's asthmatic, she told me. Did you know that?" I don't know what made me blurt it out, but there it was.

He flicked a look up at me finally, his blue eyes faintly annoyed. "I think she mentioned it once. Why?"

"Spring. Allergies. It's why she's sick. I was just..." The words trailed off.

He didn't look surprised. Or concerned. Or...well, much of anything. He just shrugged. "She can get to it when she's feeling better. There's no rush. The *Devoted* project is now front and center."

I nodded and looked down at the piles he was making. My brain was already making sense of it. I knew what he was planning and there were some who wouldn't fit for what he needed, others who were a bad risk. Those went into one pile. I'd guessed many of them, I was happy to see. A few surprised me, but there were a couple I would have pegged for that pile that didn't go.

When one of them ended up in the other pile, I went to say something and then stopped myself.

Dominic looked up. "What?"

"She..." Then I shook my head.

"If I didn't want your opinion on things, Aleena, you wouldn't be here." Some of the distance left his eyes and he crooked a smile at me.

For the first time in what felt like a lifetime, the

ice in my chest receded and I smiled back. Then I gestured at the employee data he held on one of the top matchmakers for *Devoted*. "Miriam Beckman. Are you sure you want to contact her? She's one of their top people and she..." I stopped, cleared my throat and then continued, "At one point, she was engaged to the owner."

"I know," he said mildly.

I pressed on. "She must be incredibly loyal to the company to still be working there. Are you certain you want to contact her?"

He stacked the pages, tapping them on his hand. "What makes you think these are the ones I want to contact?"

"Please." I rolled my eyes. "Two of those in the other pile recently left Eddie to work for *Devoted*. The other one changes careers more often than I change my purse."

Dominic lips curled in a smile. "You've changed your purse three times in the last five weeks, Aleena. This guy's been at *Devoted* for eighteen months."

"Before I started working for you, I used the same purse for five years." I gave him a superior look. "I never had to worry about having a different one for different occasions or outfits."

"Point made." Then he tossed the pages he held down onto the couch next to him. "Yes, I'm contacting Miriam...and the rest." He nodded to the carelessly thrown sheets of paper I'd spent the afternoon compiling into neat piles. "I've met Miri. I liked her. She doesn't pull punches and if she agrees to come in, it will be because she wants to hear what I have to say. And she won't sell me out."

He shrugged and I knew that was that.

"Sounds fair." Nodding, I went to stand.

"You did well," he murmured, looking away again.

"Thank you." I told myself I'd go up to my room, make myself something to eat, collapse into the tub. Relax. I walked four steps and then spun back to look at him. "Hey, why don't we go out?"

Dominic slowly looked up and stared at me. "Out?"

"Yeah." I managed a weak, wobbling smile. "Out. You know...for a drink. Dinner. We've never done that."

His gaze seemed to hold me hostage and I couldn't breathe, couldn't move.

Then, slowly, he shifted his attention back down to the work he had in front of him. "We can order in, Aleena. I wouldn't mind a drink, though. Do you like scotch?"

I didn't answer. Numbly, I turned away and moved into the kitchen.

I splashed some of the brand I knew he liked into a glass and carried it to him. I placed it in front of him and then called in an order to the French restaurant I knew he liked. I was thinking ice cream would be better than alcohol for how I was feeling right now.

I was nearing the top of the stairs when he called my name, but I ignored him.

Why in the hell hasn't he taken you out?

***

He came to me later that night. I'd heard him knocking on the door to my suite but didn't answer. I hadn't locked it though so he came in anyway.

I was on my side, facing away from the door.

When he moved to stand between me and the window, I was tempted to feign sleep, but I didn't have the energy.

Instead, when he crouched down in front of me, I just looked at him. I was so tired of all this.

He reached up and touched my mouth.

I turned my face away.

"What's wrong?" Dominic asked softly.

Never let it be said that Dominic Snow can't tell when a woman isn't up for sex.

"I'm not feeling well," I said honestly. Not that I was about to tell him that I felt like my heart had been ripped out of my chest and then danced on. No. Not danced on. Smashed. Ground into the cool Italian marble by the heel of his Italian leather shoes while he calmly focused on the data of his upcoming business acquisition.

Rolling onto my belly, I pressed my face into the pillow and waited for the sound of the door to close.

Instead, the mattress made a soft sighing sound as he sat down next to me. I thought he could take a hint. If I wasn't up for sex, what was the point in him hanging around? He'd made it clear that's what our relationship was. His cheap little secret.

He ran his hand over my hair and I tensed.

"Relax," he murmured.

I tensed even more.

He laid his hands on my shoulders and I gasped at the contact of his skin against mine. I was wearing a tank top, and a thin one at that. It had been days. Just a few really, but days. Too many of them. Yet the thought of being with him right now only made the misery inside me deepen.

My body didn't seem to get the message though. My nipples tightened and I tried to ignore the tug down low between my thighs. Dammit! I still wanted him.

Talented, skilled fingers dug into the muscles along my neck and shoulders.

"Relax," he said again.

I couldn't possibly...

A startled moan escaped me.

He pressed his thumbs into the muscles at the base of my neck and I shuddered. He began to work the knots with surprising skill and a few minutes later, a warm, blissful lassitude spread through me.

Before he stood, I was asleep.

"Mr. Snow will see you now." I smiled at the brunette who waited in the rose-colored, scoop styled chair.

We'd come to Philadelphia three days ago and I was exhausted. I hadn't exactly *lied* last week when I told Dominic I wasn't feeling well. I was heartsick, or at least close to it, and that didn't manifest in happy, cheerful ways, right?

The massage he'd given me had resulted in one blissful night of sleep. The last I'd had, actually. The next morning, we'd hit the ground running and it hadn't stopped since.

The phone calls had started that morning, followed by more calls, hours spent pouring over work histories and digging into backgrounds and unearthing everything I possibly could on the shortlist of the people Dominic needed to talk to at *Devoted*. On a few, I did end up using one of the investigators he'd recommended, but I did most of it myself.

This was the first time I'd be around when he instituted a takeover and I wanted to make sure everything was perfect. I couldn't let him lose it because of me.

Amber was excited.

I was too stressed to feel anything but that.

67

Two nights ago, I'd practically staggered into the suite of rooms Amber had reserved for me, but before I'd been able to close the door, Dominic had slid inside behind me.

"I thought we could have a drink, maybe dinner," he'd murmured, smoothing a hand down my arm, then curling it around my waist.

I might have been able to work up the interest, especially after he'd pressed his lips to my neck, but then he'd said the words *room service* and it was like he'd rubbed salt into an open wound.

More and more, it was starting to seem like he just didn't want to be seen in public with me. Like I was exactly what I'd always feared I'd be: the dark-skinned mistress, the exotic indulgence.

It had been easy to plead exhaustion and when he'd looked at me, I'd seen a flicker of something in his eyes, speculation, maybe something else, but there was also genuine concern. "You should rest, but make sure you eat, Aleena."

I'd told him I would. Then I went straight to bed. I couldn't have eaten anything if I tried. Not just because I'd been exhausted, but because I hadn't thought my stomach could handle it.

The past three days had been the worst, though, a blur of interviews, meetings, interviews, more meetings and hurried meals. Those meetings, meals and interviews were all taking place at the very plush accommodations offered by Masque Philadelphia, the chain of luxury hotels that Dominic owned. It had been, I'd learned, his first real business enterprise, and still his most profitable.

I had to admit, having exquisite accommodations at just about any premiere destination available at your beck and call sure as hell made life easier. As I led Miriam Beckman across the steel gray carpet, I asked her about her drive in, whether she was enjoying the spring weather. Typical, polite small talk.

Instead of answering, she gave me a direct look. "Just how many of us is Mr. Snow seeing, Ms. Davison?"

I paused in the middle of reaching for the door that led to the offices Dominic was using.

I knew I couldn't really answer that although I knew the answer. Amber and I had helped dig up and locate the information, then we'd set up the appointments with the people Dominic had decided would be ideal. But I wasn't going to pass anything on. So I just smiled. "He's speaking to people who caught his interest, Ms. Beckman."

"Hmmm..." She nodded and then fell silent as I opened the door.

Dominic was sitting behind the desk, but rose at our arrival. He barely glanced at me, offering just a polite nod, all of his interest focused on the very sharp Miriam Beckman.

I went to shut the door, but just as I started to tug on it, Dominic's gaze came to me. "Ms. Davison, I need my noon hour blocked out, absolutely no disturbances. See to it, will you?"

"Of course." Once I'd pulled the door closed, I put in a call to Amber and relayed the message. She'd stayed back in New York, working on last minute details for the upcoming dinner and fine tuning things with Eddie's assistant, Clarice. Most of the details *appeared* to be coming from Clarice at least. Couldn't have anybody thinking *Trouver L'Amour* was footing the bill, right?

Amber was also doing the initial interviews for the person who'd take over for her at the company. She'd made noises that they needed to get somebody as top dog, too. *Dominic's going to be bored here soon. I've got to get my replacement in and ready before that happens.*

Dominic and boredom didn't mix well, I suspected. And he definitely seemed the type to get bored easily.

Longing twisted inside me and I looked down the hall toward the door that separated me from him. There was more than the expanse of carpet, more than a solid door of polished oak.

Why in the hell hasn't he taken you out?

The hollow ache in my chest had become so familiar at this point, I'd almost expect to be used to it. But I wasn't. I rubbed the heel of my hand over it as I slid into my chair. My phone rang and I answered it without looking at the display, something I really knew better than to do.

The slow, southern drawl added to the headache

pounding at the base of my skull as I recognized the voice right off. I liked her, but I wasn't in the mood for cheer right now. "Annette, I hope you're feeling better."

"I am, thank you! A dose of steroids will do wonders for you," she said and I could hear the smile in her voice.

She definitely sounded better. I wondered if steroids would help a broken heart.

Broken hearts...dammit. Dammit. Damn it all to hell. I'm in love with him.

"Aleena, are you there?" She sounded concerned.

"I..." I struggled to clear my throat but couldn't. "I can't..."

Humiliation choked me and I hung up the phone, leaving it on my desk as I rushed into the small restroom tucked off to the side of the office. Pressing my back to the door, I clamped a hand over my mouth to muffle the sob.

I'm in love with him.

Rocking myself back and forth, I started to sob. It had hit me with all the force of a physical blow and I couldn't breathe.

No, no, no, no...

There was a knock at the door.

I froze.

"Aleena?"

It wasn't Dominic.

Clearing my throat, I said, "Ah...one moment." It

71

didn't sound great, but it also didn't sound like I'd just been freaking out, so that was good.

I moved to the sink and turned on the water. It wasn't until I straightened that I saw her reflection in the mirror. It was Annette Shale. With water dripping off my face, I gaped at her.

"Hi." She managed a strained smile. "I...well, damn, girl. I was in the area for an auction, picking up a few pieces for a client, and I heard you and Dominic were down here."

She sighed and moved forward, tugging a soft towel from a rod just a foot away. While I continued to stare at her, she shoved it under the water and then twisted the excess out before moving to stand in front of me. "If Dr. Annette can offer some advice?" she said softly. "What you need is ice cream and a good, long talk with a girlfriend."

"Um..." Great. I'd hoped it wasn't that obvious.

She held out the towel. "Since it's the middle of the day and I know what a pain in the ass Dominic can be to work for, you'll have to settle for this and a few ibuprofen. Take this. I'll grab the ibuprofen and meet you at your desk in a moment."

A moment was probably all I had, so I made the most of it, pressing the towel to my face and letting it cool my heated flesh. Whether it would do much for my puffy eyes, I had no idea.

Slipping out of the restroom a few minutes later, I found Annette seated in the chair Miriam had occupied. When she saw me, she rose and held out a white bottle.

I smiled weakly.

"Please tell me it's not Dominic," she said, her voice soft.

My gaze flew to hers. "You...he..."

"No." Her eyes widened and she laughed. "Oh, honey, no! That boy is almost ten years younger than I am. Plus, I'm...well...let's just say that my marriage wasn't one based on sex." She waved a hand, making it clear that wasn't part of the discussion. "You've been living with him a while and you don't strike me as a fool."

I went red.

Annette smiled and I saw the knowledge in her eyes. It wasn't snide or condescending. She just *knew*. "Dominic is a beautiful man, Aleena." She paused and then added with a partial smile, "I'm asexual, not blind."

I fiddled with the lid on the painkillers, unsure of what to say.

Annette reached out and took the bottle, twisting it open and spilling two into her palm. When she held them out, I accepted and moved to the water I'd poured myself earlier.

"If you two aren't..." I stopped, unsure how to proceed.

There was a strained, almost painful silence. I looked up when I heard her moving, her heels muffled by the plush carpet. Her red hair was pulled back in an elegant chignon, a scarf draped carelessly around her neck. She wore a silk jacket of bright purple over a white t-shirt and jeans. She looked beautiful and sexy and casual and confident. Everything I wasn't.

And her eyes were kind.

She held out a hand.

Slowly, I accepted.

"We *aren't*, and never were," she said, squeezing my fingers. "Trust me. But Dominic...that man and commitment? They don't exist. Now, he's a good man. He really is, but..." A door opened and she lapsed into silence for a moment before she sighed and spoke again, "Look, I was calling to see if you wanted to join me for lunch. We could go over some things for the penthouse and I had a few ideas for the main house, too. But fuck that. We can..."

"Annette, hello."

We both looked up to see Dominic standing in the doorway to his office, Miriam Beckman at his side.

Dominic glanced at me then back to Annette. But his gaze came right back to me, eyes narrowing slightly. He opened his mouth to say something, but then stopped himself, shaking his head.

Instead, he looked at Miriam. "Miri, it was a pleasure. I hope to hear from you soon."

"You will." She nodded at him, and the smile on her face told me that Dominic had won.

He usually did.

She smiled at me, but the smile faltered. "Are

you well, Ms. Davison?"

"I'm fine. My...ah...contact slipped." I lied. I didn't wear them.

She rolled her eyes and grimaced in sympathy. "Get the surgery. I had it ten years ago. Best decision of my life." She held out a hand and we shook. "I'll be seeing you shortly."

Then she left the three of us alone.

"I take it the meeting went well," I said, moving to my desk without looking at Dominic.

"It did. Annette, how are you?" Dominic asked. The question was more rote than anything else. He was staring at me the entire time. I could feel it, but I didn't look up.

"Much better, thank you. I'm sorry to hold things up for you. I heard you two were in town and I came to kidnap Aleena for lunch, try to get caught up. Is that okay?"

I bent to get my purse from the cabinet. "Sounds grea—"

"No. Aleena and I already have lunch plans."

Chapter 7

Dominic

Aleena stared listlessly at her desk as I walked Annette to the door.

When I turned back to study her, she didn't look up. She just sat there moving things around her desk, checking her phone, tapping at it, then putting it down. Then she started the cycle all over again. Moving the leather-bound agenda she carried everywhere. A file folder—it went back to the position it had been in sixty seconds ago.

"Enough!" I snapped when she picked up her phone the third time.

She flinched.

Then, slowly, she lowered the phone and lifted her head, staring at me for the first time since I'd come out of my office.

Her soft, pretty green eyes were dull, red-rimmed and puffy. Had she been crying?

"Aleena, what—"

The knock on the door came at the worst time and I might have just taken the head off the bastard behind it. Fortunately, I remembered at the last moment that I'd ordered lunch for us. I'd wanted to make sure she ate. I didn't think she'd been eating. She looked thinner. But I also wanted to spend some time with her. I wanted to just...

I missed her.

It hit me hard in the gut.

I *missed* her.

Not sex. Or, not only sex. I missed *her*.

I stood to the side as two men pushed in carts laden with trays. They were followed by several more men, carrying a tablecloth, a silver bucket filled with ice, bottles of wine. Everything I needed to make a perfect, romantic meal.

Aleena had risen and moved to stand by the bank of windows and she watched in silence as they set up the elegant meal I'd ordered while I waited for my interview with Miri.

Once they were gone, she glanced at me. Her eyes were no longer dull. They were frozen.

Just as cold as her words. "Of course, we're having lunch in. I'd planned on going out, but...well. Fuck that idea."

She moved to the table and before I could make myself move, she pulled out a chair and sat down.

Something's not right. That thought danced

through my mind. No shit. She never swore at work. If nothing else, that was a clear indication that she was upset.

Aleena gave me a sharp-edged smile. "Let's eat, Mr. Snow."

Shit. She was seriously pissed.

There were a few things I'd decided over the past ten days. Ten days since I'd held her against me, had her under me, felt her body vibrate as she moaned and came around me. I could count each one of them, could probably detail every last second of them, because too many seconds ticked away without her in my arms.

But those things I'd decided?

They were short and they were simple.

I missed her.

There were things in my life that were expected of me. Up until recently, I hadn't thought much of them. I'd just accepted them.

It was like the sky was blue, even when the clouds hid it.

The sun would rise.

I was rich.

And it was expected that I would marry or at least cohabitate with a socially acceptable female. Gotta carry on the family name somehow, right?

But...I didn't want to.

A socially acceptable female was somebody like Penelope Harrington, and if I had to come home to that bitch even one night, I knew I'd walk in front of a speeding SUV with my arms spread out. I'd welcome the ugly, messy death, because at least that would be fast. Any sort of life with Penelope would be a slow, miserable death. She would suck every bit of me out, and I don't mean in the hot and sexy way that involved her mouth and any kind of pleasure on my part *or* hers.

Socially acceptable. Duty. Expectation.

Those lay in one direction and I knew it.

The woman in front of me was something else entirely, and I was starting to realize that she was the last sort of woman I needed in my life. But she might also be the only woman who ever mattered.

She wouldn't stand calmly and aloofly at my side as I discussed my next business deal. When cutting remarks were made about class or race among those in my social circle, as they often were, Aleena would cut back. And she'd make damn sure everybody in listening distance heard just how idiotic and shallow they all came across.

Now, she sat across the table from me in silence, twisting her fork in the pasta I'd ordered for lunch, her eyes meeting mine with cool defiance. The one thing I wanted more than anything was to knock the whole fucking table out of the way and grab her, shove her skirt up and pull her down on my cock.

She was mine.

With a clarity unlike anything I'd ever known, I knew that one thing.

Aleena was mine.

It took all the patience I had to eat maybe half of the food on my plate. Then I leaned back and sipped from the wine I'd selected. She wouldn't choose. I'd brought in four different wine selections, all vintages I knew she liked, but she had just shrugged them off and refused to show any interest, so I went with the one I thought she'd enjoyed the most.

She'd had maybe three sips.

She'd eaten four bites of pasta and pushed the food around.

Finally, she put the fork down and stopped even pretending to eat, leveling me a look that should have pissed me off. If she had been anybody other than who she was, I would've been hard-pressed to keep my temper.

If I had to put a caption on that look, it would've been simple: *Bite Me.*

I was tempted to do just that.

"I've been thinking..." I put the glass of wine down and tossed my napkin beside it.

Aleena lifted a brow. Her voice was coolly professional. "Should I get my planner?"

"No." I wouldn't rise to the bait. There was no reason. "This isn't related to business. It's personal."

"Oh, really?"

Aleena's eyes narrowed as she studied me. The moment stretched out and I felt like a microbe caught between slides, examined by her. Refusing to let her get under my skin, I hooked one ankle over my knee and gave her a cocky smile. "We never have really talked about...us."

I expected a reaction from that.

The good thing about expectations? If you have them, they are almost always met.

The bad thing? They are rarely met in the way you hoped.

Aleena stared at me for a long minute, and then she shook her head and started to laugh.

That laugh echoed. Through the silence of the office, off the walls and back to my ears. It echoed and rang and the only way I was able to sit there and not react was because I'd had too many fucking years of *not* reacting, of not allowing myself the luxury of reacting.

But it was an effort.

That laugh was jagged and harsh, full of mockery and misery and loathing. But I couldn't tell who it was directed at. Herself...or me.

"Us?" she finally said. Aleena leaned forward and grabbed the glass of wine that had been put in front of her nearly thirty minutes earlier. She drank half of it and then put the glass down.

"*Us*?" she repeated, staring at me with speculation. "Exactly what *us* do you mean, Dominic? There *is* no us."

"Of course there is," I snapped.

She surged upright then, moving with such speed that she sent the wine glass flying. Drops of ruby red splattered on the floor, but she didn't even look. Her pale green eyes locked on mine and she sneered at me. "*Us*? Oh, bite me, Dominic. The only *us* that exists is the *us* that suits you. You want me in your fucking bed—excuse the pun there. That's *it*. Now, if you don't mind, I'd like a *real* break before we get back to the interviews—"

She'd delivered those words as she strode to the door, the final words said over her shoulder. Before she could open the door, I slammed my hand against it.

She turned and glared at me. "Do you *mind*?"

"Yes." Then I jerked her up against me and slanted my mouth over hers.

She didn't respond.

Just then, I didn't care. I would make her react. I knew she wanted me.

She went to shove me away and I caught her wrists, dragged them over her head, my lips forcing hers apart. When I traced my tongue along her bottom lip, she shuddered.

"Tell me you don't want this," I whispered against her mouth. Slowly, I lifted my head and stared down into her eyes.

She was panting, her breath coming in hard, labored gasps. I could feel each ragged, unsteady rise and fall. I could feel her nipples, even through the layers of her bra and blouse, through my own clothes. Still watching her, I lifted a hand and cupped her breast, peering into her eyes as I circled the swollen peak with my thumb. "You don't want this?"

"You son of a bitch," she said, her voice rough. "You know I do."

I caught the hem of her skirt and dragged it up.

She wore stockings, the kind that ended high on her thigh. I toyed with the wide band of lace, traced the edge with my fingers before I caught the thin strip of cotton that covered her crotch. A miserable excuse for panties. A woman like her should be wearing silk and lace. She whimpered as I ran my finger across the damp material. Tugging it out of the way, I bent my head and whispered into her ear, "Unzip me, Aleena."

For a few seconds, the world froze. Nothing happened.

Then, I felt her fingers moving between us and fire flooded me, arcing between us as she slid her hand inside my open fly and freed me, wrapping her hand around my cock and stroking. Up, down, up, down...I didn't realize I was blindly pumping into her touch until a warning jolt of pleasure raced down my spine.

Snarling, I caught her hand and shoved it over her head. Not like that.

Her eyes were wide. Slowly, I bent my knees to accommodate for the difference in our height and then, angling my hips, I waited for consent. I would push her, but I would never truly force her. I could never do that to anyone, let alone someone I–

She caught my cock and guided me to her entrance.

I drove in, deep, hard and fast. Home.

She shuddered and brought up one knee.

I caught the other and lifted her. She clung to me as I carried her across the room, over to the table. My cock was painfully hard, my body begging me to thrust, to lose myself in her.

I swept one arm out, knocking dishes and glasses aside. Dishes went flying. Wine splattered and then I put her down, spread her out just the way I'd imagined. A drop of ruby red wine clung to her cheek, another on her lip, several on her neck and chest.

I licked each one way as I thrust deep and hard inside her.

"You." I drove into her. "Are." Again. "Mine."

Aleena closed her eyes, turning her face away from me.

I cupped her chin, making her face me. "Look at me."

Slowly, her lashes lifted.

"Mine." When she didn't respond, I bent down and bit her lip. She shuddered and I felt the wet, snug grip of her pussy tighten around my dick. "Say it, Aleena."

She arched against me. Her voice broke as she whispered, "Yes, sir."

It wasn't what I wanted.

But in the moment, it was enough.

***

"We should discuss where this is going."

Aleena stood with her back to me, adjusting her clothing. Her hands hesitated only a second and then she glanced over her shoulder. "And where is it going, Dominic?"

I miss you.

The words were right there.

They really were.

I wanted to tell her.

I could even hear myself saying it.

I thought I could even see the way her eyes would soften. She'd reach for me. We could...

The phone rang.

Its shrill ring shattered the silence and I looked away. Neither of us moved to answer it, but it didn't matter. Clearing my throat, I finished adjusting my clothes. "We both want things outside a business relationship, Aleena. We'd be lying to ourselves if we tried to pretend otherwise."

Aleena, her back to me, didn't acknowledge my words.

I wanted to press my lips to the elegant curve where neck gave way to spine.

I wanted to cup my hands around her breasts, pull her against me and tell her whatever she wanted to hear.

86

Instead, I waited in silence.

"Let's not lie to ourselves, right, Dominic?" she said, her voice oddly empty.

I had the feeling I was still missing something. "We both want the same thing. Each other."

"The same thing. Of course." She nodded and went into the restroom to finish cleaning up.

Something was still wrong. I walked past her as she came out of the bathroom and I closed the door behind me, confused and, despite what had happened, unsatisfied. She was at the table, setting it to rights when I came out of the small restroom.

"Leave it," I said irritably.

"It won't take long." She shrugged and righted a wine glass, placed a plate and a serving dish in its former place. "I—"

"The party at Eddie's."

She glanced at me, her lips in a flat line. "Amber has everything ready, of course."

Out. You know...for a drink. Dinner. We've never done that.

Her words from last week rang in my ears. I don't know why. But they did.

The dull look in her eyes, followed by ice.

Of course, we're having lunch in. I'd planned on going out, but...well. Fuck that idea.

"I've got a number of things to get done before the next appointment arrives," Aleena said, skirting to go around me. "And I'm sure there are things you need to do."

I caught her wrist. "I thought perhaps you and I could attend Eddie's party...together."

"I wasn't planning on doing anything more than making a work-required appearance. I wouldn't want to take away from your fun."

Pieces fell into place. Every time she'd tried to get us to go out somewhere, I'd shut her down, wanted to stay in. Because I hadn't wanted to share her. But she didn't think that. She thought I didn't want anyone to know we were together.

"I'd prefer to have you there with me the whole time."

Aleena's eyes flew to mine and she stumbled, all but crashing into my chest. My arms automatically went out to catch her and I couldn't help but think how naturally we fit together.

She looked surprised, but still wary. I managed a smile and had to clarify my previous statement. I wasn't ashamed to be with her, but I wasn't making some sort of commitment either. "It's a dinner party, Aleena. We both have to attend. Why not go together?"

Chapter 8

Aleena

Why not go together?

Easy question, right?

Except when I still didn't know what 'together' meant.

Now, after all those days of brooding and wondering why we hadn't ever gone out on a date, here I was, standing in front of a mirror, brushing makeup onto my eyelids and half-wishing I'd told Dominic to find somebody else.

Somebody like...oh, Penelope Rittenour.

She would have loved to have gone to this party with Dominic. I could practically see her picking out wedding patterns. In the past couple of weeks, Dominic and I had traveled back and forth between New York and Philadelphia so often, I felt like I was running into my own shadow and when I wasn't running into *my* shadow, I was running into hers.

She seemed to have developed a radar and knew

exactly when to be in the New York office, coming in just as we were or leaving a nearby spa just as we happened by. She'd dropped heavy hints about spending a day in Philadelphia and it would be so lovely to have some companionship.

I, of course, had been completely ignored during these conversations. I hadn't really minded, not wanting to waste the breath it would have taken to speak to her.

The phone rang, pulling me out of my thoughts and I took the call, putting Molly on speaker so I could finish my makeup.

"You haven't gone and chickened out yet?" Molly asked. I chuckled under my breath and Molly laughed. "Come on. You've been wanting him to ask you out on a real date and now he's doing it. Why are you so nervous?"

We'd been up until midnight talking. I'd thought it would help settle the nerves. It hadn't.

"I don't know," I said, sighing. Straightening, I studied my reflection, angling my head left, then right. I'd made an appointment with a stylist the concierge had recommended. I hardly ever bothered paying somebody to do my hair, but this dinner party was important. Besides, I'd hoped the small bit of pampering would make me relax.

It hadn't.

But at least my hair looked damned good, smooth and straight, pulled up and back into a complicated twist that I'd never have been able to manage on my own. Butterflies, bunny rabbits and buffalos seemed to be dancing around in my belly and I pressed my hand to it, hoping they'd get the point and settle down.

"I should have said no." Hindsight was such a bitch. "I mean, come on, Moll. He didn't really ask me *out*. He was pointing out the fact that both of us had to go and that he'd want me there the whole time. Of course he'd need me there. It's an important business venture."

"You're being stupid. Of course you're both working. If he didn't want you to think of it as a date or anything, he just wouldn't have said anything about it. He wanted to make sure *you* knew it was a date and wasn't planning to bring anybody." Molly explained everything with the same tone she'd use when talking to an idiot.

Rolling my eyes at the phone, I thought about arguing with her and pointing out all the holes in that argument. But I caught sight of the time. Groaning, I said, "I need to finish getting ready."

"Oh, please do...hey, I'm hanging up. Wait! Face-time! I wanna see your dress."

I went to argue, but she'd already hung up. The phone chimed again and when Molly's face appeared on the phone, I made a face at her.

She wolf-whistled at me when I put the phone back down and turned to get my dress. "Love the panties, Aleena. So much sexier than what you usually wear!"

I ignored her and tugged the dress off the hanger.

I'd found it online a few weeks ago and bought it on a whim. It wasn't a designer piece—or, well, it was, but not the sort of designer piece that Fawna had taken me shopping for. It was a retro-styled ivory silk wiggle dress and thanks to the built-in shape-wear, it fit like a dream and outlined every curve I had.

It took some wiggling to get into it and I was grimacing by the time I smoothed it into place. "I wonder if that's where the name for the stupid design came from," I muttered, turning around and looking into Molly's grinning face.

"I feel like I should be tucking a dollar into your bra or something," she said.

"Pervert." I stuck my tongue out and looked at my reflection. "How do I look?"

"Like some starlet straight out of the glamour days of Hollywood."

I glanced at the phone and quirked an eyebrow at Molly.

She made a little *X* over her chest. "Cross my heart. You look amazing. I wish I had the *T* and *A* for that sort of style."

"*T* and *A*?"

"Tits and ass, girl." Molly wiggled her eyebrows at me. "You're going to knock him dead."

Sighing, I went back to studying myself in the mirror. I'd swiped out the chain on my grandmother's necklace for a slightly longer one, leaving the pendant to nestle between my breasts but I looked...bare. The dress lay low on my shoulders and while my skin glowed softly against the ivory silk, I felt like I needed something else.

I didn't have anything though.

"Aleena?"

"Yes?" I asked absently.

"Try to have fun, okay?"

"Yeah." I smiled, but it looked as fake as it felt. This was going to be a disaster. I knew it. "Of course, I'll have fun."

***

I had the suite across from Dominic's.

Our two rooms were the only ones on the top floor. His was the presidential suite, although *palatial* would probably have been more accurate.

Mine wasn't anything to sneer at though and I wished I'd had the time to appreciate it more, but as it was, the only thing I'd done was collapse on the lake-size bed or collapse into the lake-size Jacuzzi tub or watch TV from the massive couch. That is, when I wasn't working my ass off, which had been ninety-nine percent of the time.

Right now, I was standing at the window,

staring out over the skyline of Philadelphia. It was so different from New York. They were both old cities, but so much of the new in New York had swallowed up the old. In Philadelphia, they blended. Two things that should have been at odds, that shouldn't have looked right side-by-side, came together in this wonderful, enchanting city.

I pressed a hand to the glass, warmed by the sun and tried to will away the tension knotting my shoulders.

Dominic had told me that he'd like to leave at five. The party started at seven, but he wanted to go over everything with Eddie and have time to get his pieces in position. I wondered if he liked to play chess.

The door to my suite opened. Dominic. He had a copy of my room key. Tucked inside my wallet, I had a copy of his too. Not that I'd felt inclined to use it. Things still felt so unsettled between us. I felt uneasy and the sensation grew as his gaze settled on the nape of my neck.

Slowly, I shifted my attention to the wavy reflection the window provided. I could just barely see Dominic's outline, but I didn't need to see him to know what he was doing. He was watching me. When he started toward me, my heart skipped a beat and then started to race.

He stopped just a few inches behind me and rested a hand on the curve of my waist. "You look lovely."

"Thank you."

"Part of me wants to tug on this zipper..."

I shivered as his fingers brushed the tab.

"Peel this dress off of you and bend you over." Dominic murmured the words into my ear. As he did so, he took one of my hands and pressed it to the glass. "This way..."

He caught the other hand and guided it into place and then nudged me low. "I could take you like this."

I shuddered as I felt him rub his cock against my covered ass.

"But I think I'll wait until tonight."

The hand he'd put on my waist slid around and I gasped when he pressed two fingers against me. Involuntarily, I shuddered and rocked against him, drawing out a slow, startled moan. He rubbed me through my clothing, teasing me, taunting me.

When I started to pant, his motions grew quicker, and panic cut through arousal. Abruptly, I pulled away. Moving a few feet to the side, I looked down at my hands. They were shaking.

"The party," I reminded him.

He rubbed at his top lip with his right hand, his eyes burning, pupils wide. "The party." His gaze slid across me, the heat in it so powerful, I felt as though he'd physically ran his hands over me. He reached inside his coat and held out a box. "A gift. I saw your dress and thought you might wear this with it."

I lowered my eyes and stared at the box. It was

flat and white. White velvet, I realized, as I slowly took it from him. I gasped when I flipped open the lid.

What lay inside knocked the breath right out of me.

Diamonds. They sparkled like stars on a bed of gleaming metal and my fingers itched to touch, but I didn't dare.

Snapping the box shut, I said, "I can't accept this." I pushed it back toward him.

"You can," he insisted as he took the box.

I figured out why quickly enough. He took the necklace out and came to stand behind me, the jewels held in his hands. He put it on my neck with the skill of a man who'd done that sort of thing more than once.

"Dominic, I can't wear this," I said weakly.

"Yes, you can." He trailed a finger along my neck, under the chain that held my grandmother's necklace. He carefully unlatched it and set it aside. "You wear this one. Wearing another necklace is no different."

"My grandmother's necklace doesn't have diamonds on it the size of grapes!" I turned and glared at him.

He seemed to have been waiting for just that.

Before I'd even realized what was happening, I was pressed between him and the window, and his tongue was in my mouth. Fuck. I couldn't think straight when he was touching me. Despite the fact that I had so many reservations, that I had questions that needed answers, desire flooded me and I curled my tongue around his and sucked.

He curved his hand around my neck, his thumb pressing into the hollow in the base. He pulled back and murmured against my lips. "I want you to do that with my cock in your mouth."

His blue eyes glittered down at me and I shuddered. Licking my lips, I tried to think of what to say, but he pulled back, the reluctance clear on his face.

"We need to go. Now." His gaze slid over me and my nipples tightened, chafing against my bra. "Otherwise, we won't be going anywhere." He didn't step back though. Instead, he turned his face into my hair and said softly, "I'm going to spend half the night thinking about that, Aleena. How it will feel when I finally have you on your knees in front of me, taking my cock into your mouth, one slow inch at a time."

My mouth went dry.

It didn't dawn on me until later that I'd completely forgotten to keep arguing with him about the necklace.

***

"Well, isn't this...lovely?"

That voice grated on my ears and I was glad I'd had my back turned when she approached. Next to me, Dominic stiffened and I saw the surprise in his eyes when he looked at the woman who'd just descended the stairs of the hotel's grand ballroom.

Eddie White, from what Dominic had told me, had been in the matchmaking game almost since before such a thing existed. He'd been one of the pioneers, quick, clever, and thorough. And somehow, it appeared that Penelope Rittenour had managed to con her way into being one of his few guests.

Eddie had given us the final headcount just a few days ago, told us the names of all the key personnel and mentioned while most of his people were married and would be bringing their spouses, a few would be coming alone or bringing significant others. We were just going over the list now and I saw she'd been added, her name glared at me from the bottom of the page.

"Penelope," Dominic said, his tone neutral.

That didn't slow her down. She continued her slow, sensual glide down the steps, never once looking away from Dominic's face. It was like I didn't even exist.

"I must say, I'm surprised to see you here," Dominic said when she came to a stop in front of the small table where we had been discussing a few last minute details.

"Dominic." Penelope touched her tongue to her lower lip. She wore a deep, deep shade of red on her pretty mouth, just a few shades darker than the dress she wore. The red was stunning against her ivory complexion and I had to admit, she looked amazing. Slowly, she slid her tongue along the curve of her lip and then she smiled and cocked her head to the side. "It's wonderful to see you."

"As I said, it's surprising to see you."

"Well." Her lashes fell to shield her eyes for a moment and then she looked back at him. "I'd mentioned I had business here. I ran into Eddie and heard about his dinner party. When he mentioned you'd be here..." Her gaze slid to me and then away. "I'd love if we could have some time to talk. Alone. Eddie said you hadn't made plans to bring a date."

The bottom of my stomach clutched and then fell out.

"Eddie's mistaken." Dominic touched his hand to my lower back. "Aleena's my companion tonight, Penelope."

His thumb swept along my spine, burning through my dress. I clutched at the folder I'd been holding, staring blindly at Penelope.

Aleena's my companion...

Penelope seemed to have the same trouble processing those words as I did, but I wasn't sure it was for the same reason. Companion. Not date. Not lover or girlfriend. Companion.

What the hell did that mean?

Penelope laughed.

It was an overly loud, almost braying sort of noise that made the work going on us around fall silent for the briefest of moments. She didn't notice or care. "I'm sorry. You didn't..." She laughed again, but it was quieter, like she'd gathered herself. She shook her head and leaned closer, as though the table between us and the distance of two feet might account for some of her confusion. "It seemed like you said you brought your *secretary* as your date. Dominic, your sense of humor has been very strange lately."

"Aleena isn't my secretary," Dominic said. He looked down at me. "We'll need to wrap this up elsewhere." He turned back to Penelope. "And I'm afraid I don't see what amuses you or strikes you as humorous about my choice of company."

While she continued to gape at us, Dominic gathered up the pages we'd been studying and then held out his hand. Feeling strangely numb, I accepted.

***

"Now just where has Dominic been keeping you?"

The voice was low, full of the kind of warning

that preceded the kind of leering I'd gotten used to from certain people and the alcohol it floated on was almost enough to make *me* feel lightheaded.

We were two hours into the so-called party.

The senior staff at *Devoted* were standing around with fake smiles. The man in front of me was the son of some CEO and when he reached out to trace his finger down my arm, I backed away.

"Oh, don't be like that," he slurred. He leaned in a little closer and reached out, brushing his hand down my arm. When the heel of his hand grazed my breast, his smile widened and we both knew it wasn't an accident.

This time, I didn't put just a step between us.

I put a few feet.

He chuckled and skimmed me with a look that made me feel dirty. "I bet you're just as sweet as sugar...brown sugar, no doubt. Brown and rich and sweet and..."

I didn't let myself cringe or even cross my arms as a shield against his lecherous gaze. Instead, I gave him a cold glare. "You're about as original as you are sober, and witty too. How observant of you to notice that I'm *brown*, Mr. Pence."

He blinked at me, surprised.

"Is this the part where I'm supposed to stammer and get nervous or self-conscious? Or just be quiet while you make crude remarks to me?" I asked. "After all, isn't that my place?"

"Aleena!" Penelope gasped.

I had *no* idea where she'd come from and I turned my head, glaring at her.

"Really, that is hardly the way to talk to one of Mr. Snow's future business partners," she said, glaring down her nose at me.

"Actually, he's one of Mr. Snow's future *subordinates*," I said, watching as she hooked an arm through Mitchell Pence's. I knew Dominic wouldn't want it coming out like this, but my nerves had been stretched to the breaking point and this made them snap. "They didn't have a merger. The Winter Corporation is buying *Devoted* and rebranding it as the nest branch of *Trouver L'Amour*. There's a difference."

Pence's face went an ugly shade of red. "You stupid black bitch—"

"I'll handle this, Mitch," Penelope said softly, patting his arm. She leaned in and whispered something into his ear. The two of them were quiet a moment and then he gave a low, dirty laugh, his eyes moving to rest on the bodice of my dress as Penelope turned her gaze back to me.

"Regardless of the details of the *acquisition*, Mr. Pence is a pillar of this community who deserves more respect than you seem to be capable of giving him, Ms. Davison. Perhaps—"

"Respect?" Crossing my arms over my chest to keep me from slapping her, I took a few steps towards her. I didn't particularly *want* to be closer to either of them, but I preferred keep my voice down and still make sure she heard what I had to say. "Tell me...just how much *respect* should I show a man who invades my personal space and makes lewd comments toward me, Ms. Rittenour?"

She sniffed. "You receive the respect you earn in this life, and since we all know the real reason you're here—"

"You are..." I shook my head. "You know what. You're not even worth it." I turned and walked away.

I just wanted to get out of there.

I found something of a refuge near the patio doors that opened out into the night. Miriam Beckman was there with her husband and she smiled at me with a guarded warmth. "I think it went rather well, all things considering," she said when I paused to say hello.

"I think so too."

She made introductions and we chatted for a few minutes, the banality of the conversation allowing me to relax a bit. After her husband, a man she'd introduced as Kurt, glanced past me for the third time, I finally followed his gaze and saw Mitchell Pence leaning up against a wall nearby, staring at me.

"If your boss is even half as smart as he seems to be, the first thing he needs to do is fire that son of a bitch," Kurt said, his voice blunt.

"Kurt, please don't start," Miri said, shaking her head. "Not here."

"He's a dick, Miri. A dangerous one."

103

"Is everything okay?" I asked.

"Yes, of course," Miri said, clearly lying through her teeth.

Kurt said, "No." He gave me a mockery of a smile and then tilted his half-empty wine glass in Pence's direction. "That man there? He's a lawsuit waiting to happen. And if I ever see him within ten feet of Miri again, I'll rip his balls off."

It took twenty minutes to get the story out of them and my head was pounding by the time they were done. Miri looked humiliated, stressed and frustrated. Kurt was pissed. And now I had to tell Dominic that a CEO's son, one of the men we'd agreed to keep on as part of the deal, had a long, quiet history of sexual harassment.

Perfect, I thought. Outside, alone at a table by myself, I watched the party going on through the windows. The dinner was done and everybody was socializing, the feeling of relief almost palpable. We'd managed to keep a lid on everything pretty well, but those in management who'd agreed to come over with us had been walking on eggshells as they waited for Dominic to make his move. Now they could all breathe again.

Through the window, I could see Dominic talking to Eddie. I had to admit, he'd done a damn good job. Eddie looked pleased. Happy, really. He could retire at his own pace now knowing that his company and his people would be taken care of.

The door slid open.

I almost got up and left. There was another door inside, but I would damned if I let Penelope think she could chase me off.

So I stayed where I was, idly swaying to the music that played softly from hidden speakers and counting down the minutes until Dominic decided we could leave. That hot tub in my room was sounding really good right now.

Penelope said nothing right away, just came over and sat down on the opposite side of the table. Almost five minutes passed before she finally spoke, "I understand why he's attracted to you, Aleena. You really are very pretty."

I could almost hear her adding some sort of clarification. I turned my head and looked at her. "Am I supposed to say thank you?"

"I hardly expect you to have any sort of proper manners." She looked unconcerned with my response. "You're attractive and probably a unique change. After all, Dominic's lovers all tend to be from his world."

"So, Dominic's slumming with me." I gave her a hard look. "You're hardly the first to point that out. His mother beat you to it, Penelope."

Her eyes flickered and I smiled. "She told you about that, huh?"

"You're so crude." She wrinkled her nose. Then she sighed. "I don't know why I'm bothering to discuss anything with you. Have fun with him while you can, Aleena. He'll tire of you soon enough and

I'll be there waiting, as I always am. He knows where he can find me when he gets bored of you."

Bored. Dominic did get bored easily.

She rose and turned to go, but then, slowly, she turned back to face me. "I've always been there for him. I'm the one he turns to when things are the darkest when he's lost and confused. When he's hurting, he knows I'll be there. He always comes back to me. You? You're just a passing fancy."

I stared at her. "He always comes back to you? Uh-huh. Sure." I waved a dismissive hand and went back to staring in at the party. "I think it's clear how much he needs you."

Silence, heavy and weighted, fell and after a moment, I turned to look at her.

She was staring at me, a glimmer of icy amusement on her face.

"And does he need *you*, Aleena?" She glanced toward the window and then started back toward me. "Tell me, when he's hurting in the night, when the nightmares are the worst, do you know why? Do you have any idea what to say to make them go away?"

I'd been sure there was nothing she could say that would get to me any more than she already had.

I'd been wrong.

The nightmares.

I could still hear the sounds he'd made that night. The first night we'd ever had sex, it had been because I'd woken him from a nightmare. I'd never asked him what it was about and he never offered.

She leaned down, braced one hand on the table. "You *do* know about the nightmares, don't you, Aleena?" She paused and then added, "Unless of course he doesn't allow you to share his bed. He might fuck you, he does have needs, after all. I know that. But there's a difference between sex and what I can give him."

She gave me a knowing smile and then turned.

I never saw her leave.

I was too busy staring at Dominic.

***

She's just trying to get to you.

I spent twenty minutes trying to convince myself of that. I spent another ten minutes working up the courage to go inside again.

Finally, I had no choice when that ass Mitchell Pence came out.

Swallowing back the bile and fighting a headache, I made my way in and I would have found a dark, quiet corner, but Eddie saw me and caught my arm, guiding me back into the thick of things. "Everything's going wonderfully," he said, squeezing my elbow. "Dominic's been amazing. And both you and Amber have done so much...I can't thank you

107

enough."

I smiled at him.

It couldn't have been a very good effort because he paused and studied me. "Are you feeling okay, Ms. Davison?" he asked.

"I'm fine," I said. "Just tired."

"Of course. I'll..." He paused and then said, "Why don't we find you a drink? The champagne is..."

I stopped, not hearing the rest of what he said.

In front of me, not even ten feet away, Penelope was talking to Dominic. He had his back to me. She stood at an angle, facing away, their heads pressed close together. As I watched, she reached up and touched his cheek. Dominic averted his head, but didn't pull away. Penelope settled her hand on his shoulder instead, smoothing it up and down in a possessive gesture.

"I..." Swallowing, I glanced over at Eddie. "You know, I think I should go back to the hotel. I'm not feeling well."

He squeezed my hand, casting a knowing look at Penelope. "You shouldn't let her run you off, Ms. Davison."

"Oh, I'm not..." The words faded, my protest dying in my throat as I met the man's kind eyes. Finally, I cleared my throat and said, "I *am* tired."

"Of course. Allow me to get you a car at least. I'll let Dominic know you weren't feeling well." Then his eyes narrowed on Penelope, clear dislike on his face.

"Once he's done with his conversation, of course."

I nodded and he guided me away, his hand resting solicitously on my back.

***

My head was still pounding almost an hour later when I came out of the shower.

I'd hoped it would help, but it hadn't.

The sight of the man standing in the middle of my bedroom didn't help either.

Chapter 9

Aleena

Dominic stood there staring at me, looking almost too beautiful for words.

Rumpled blond hair fell across his forehead while blue eyes studied my face. The elegant tux he wore fit him to perfection, although at some point since I'd last seen him, he'd loosened his tie and it hung open at his throat, the top two buttons of his shirt freed as well.

My heart hurt just to look at him.

"Eddie said you weren't feeling well."

Turning away, I rubbed the heel of my hand over my chest. "No. I'm not."

His heavy sigh filled the room around me. "May I ask what's wrong?"

*My heart's breaking. I don't know what to think. I'm trying to figure out if I know you at all...*I wanted to tell him all of that, but I didn't know how to even begin. Taking a deep breath, I let it out slowly and then turned to face him, wondering if I had the strength to even try.

The remote look in his eyes froze every single word that came to my mind. Lamely, I said, "I've got a horrible headache."

Dominic tipped his head back, staring up at the ceiling. "A headache?"

"Yes." It was nothing less than the truth, but it was lame and I knew it. I could have stayed. I could have toughed it out if it wasn't for one little thing. Or rather, if it wasn't for one major bitch by the name of Penelope, I would have been fine. Did I have a headache? Yes. It was brought on by the stress of the party and too little sleep and just being unfamiliar with everything I was doing, but I could have popped a few Tylenol, dealt with it and pushed on.

But I wasn't going to deal with her goading me, stabbing at me, going out of her way to embarrass me at every turn.

And the uncertainty.

That was the worst of it.

Dominic had said we needed to talk, but maybe I shouldn't have avoided it. We should have talked and we hadn't and now I was left not knowing where I stood with him.

The turmoil of my thoughts was interrupted by Dominic's voice, brusque, almost harsh.

"Aleena, I realize this life is different from what you're used to, but sometimes, you're going to have to deal with shit. Headaches, feeling like shit, even rude people like Mitchell Pence."

I jerked my head up and stared at him.

"Excuse me?"

He rubbed the back of his neck. "I heard he was being a dick. I'm going to assume that has something to do with your headache."

"Something? Sure." I tightened the belt on my robe and moved past him, staring outside. I could've explained, but I decided to see how things played out. I still didn't know what Penelope had said. "Just exactly what did you hear about him, Dominic?"

"He made a move on you, didn't he?"

I slanted a look at him. "You could say that."

His jaw went tight. "I'll deal with him, Aleena. But you're a beautiful woman—"

"I'm a beautiful *black* woman, Dominic." Turning back to him, I held out my hands and said, "I'm sure you've noticed since everyone else in your life has. I'm half-black. Most of the world looks at me and sees a black woman. Period. You do understand that?"

"Yeah." He braced his hands on his hips. "Look, Aleena, that's got nothing to do—"

"That son of a bitch put his hands on me," I said. I stormed over to him and jabbed him in the chest. "So guess what, Dominic? You don't get to stand there and tell me it's got nothing to with jackshit."

He caught my wrist.

I jerked back. "Let me go," I warned him. "I've had it with people putting their hands on me today."

Dominic lowered his gaze and slowly, he let go. He didn't move back though and I could feel tension radiating off of him. "What are you talking about?" he asked quietly.

"What, didn't Penelope fill you in on all the details?" He didn't respond and I laughed, shaking my head. "So I'm right, aren't I? She decided to tell you how difficult I was being." Bitterness choked me. "I guess I should be grateful that you gave me some benefit and at least assumed he was being an asshole."

He wasn't even looking at me now and I started to walk away.

"Aleena, would you please..." He stopped and then after a moment, he tried again. "I want to know what happened."

"Sure. I'll tell you." I turned around. "That prick you agreed to take on? He called me brown sugar and a black bitch and he put his hands on me. You're fucking lucky I didn't deck him right there. And then that bitch of a girlfriend of yours had the nerve to tell me to show him respect."

I went into my bedroom and slammed the door shut. I couldn't stay here.

The party was over. Tomorrow, we were heading back. Fuck that.

I was going to figure out a way to get back to New York tonight, even if I had to rent a car and drive back myself. I couldn't stay here another minute.

The door opened and I spun around, glaring at Dominic.

"Get out!" I shouted at him. "I am so sick of you walking in whenever you feel like it!"

He flinched, but didn't move. "I'm sorry I didn't knock, but I didn't think you'd let me in."

"Damn right," I muttered.

"I needed you to hear this," he continued. "Penelope isn't my girlfriend. I can barely stand the woman."

"Sure." Misery crashed and stormed inside me as I grabbed some clothes from the dresser. "That's why she knows more about you than I do."

"Penelope doesn't know anything about me."

He blocked me when I tried to go around him.

"Yeah?" Angling my head back, I stared up at him. I clung to the clothes I held like they were somehow keeping me from falling apart. "Fine. Tell me about your nightmares."

He jerked back as if I'd slapped him.

"Okay." I nodded. That settled it then. "Okay," I repeated. I ducked around him. "This...this isn't working for me, Dominic. I think you're going to have to find a new assistant. I'm going to find someplace else..." My voice cracked and I all but tore the door open, shuddering and shaking. Tears blinded me.

"Aleena, wait."

I lunged for the bathroom. I had to get away from him.

"You are *not* leaving me."

He caught me, pulling me against him. I bucked and thrashed, trying to get out of his embrace, but he was too strong.

"Let me go!" I shouted.

His lips pressed against my cheek, while against my back, I felt the ragged rise and fall of his chest. "I can't," he whispered. "I can't...Aleena, you're mine. Don't you get it?"

"Yours?" I started to cry. So that was how he saw me then. A thing. A possession. I sagged and he caught me, lowering us both to the floor.

"Stop, please, baby," he murmured, speaking softly into my hair. "Don't cry. Don't cry..."

"I can't do this. I can't..."

"Aleena." He rubbed his cheek against mine. "I need you. I—"

"Stop saying that!" The words infuriated me and I started to fight him again, preferring anger to hurt.

I drove my head back. Pain lit inside the back of my head and he cursed, but it didn't stop me. Jerking against his hold, I reared and twisted and managed to get away, but instead of taking advantage of it, I turned and struck out, slapping him hard enough to leave a red mark on his cheek. I raised my hand again and he caught my wrists, jerking me back down on his lap.

"Stop." The word came out of him in a ragged burst. "You're going to hurt yourself. Just...just stop."

"I'm trying to hurt you, you son of a bitch! You *need* me?" I said it mockingly, letting the misery inside me drip out in each and every word. "You don't *need* me. The only thing you want from me is sex, Dominic. You said it yourself. I'm *yours*. Something to be used when you want it and discarded when you get bored."

His hands fell away and he looked at me, a look of stunned surprise on his face. "No." He shook his head. "That's...no, Aleena."

I clambered to my feet.

The red mark on his cheek looked like my hand.

The back of my head hurt and I realized, dully, that his nose was bleeding. I'd done that. He swiped his wrist under his nose and looked at the smear of blood left there. For a moment, he just stared and then lowered his hand. "No," he said again, but the word was faint. "How can you...?"

"Do you realize that we've spent more than a month together and you never once took me out on a date?" I said softly. The fury was leaving me just as quickly as it had come on. "And tonight? You said we might as well go together. Like I was some convenient option. You called me your 'companion'." I gave him a sad smile. "At least 'friend' would've implied some amount of respect. And you wouldn't have had to pretend to not be ashamed of me, because we all know that it's okay to be 'just friends'."

Chapter 10

Dominic

I didn't think anything she could have said would have hit me in the gut quite so hard. "You think I'm *ashamed* of you?"

Blood dripped down the back of my throat.

My face hurt from where she'd slapped me.

But all of that paled compared to the gaping hole that was forming inside me as I realized just how badly I'd messed up.

Eddie had told me to be careful. He'd told me she was hurting and something wasn't right. The old bastard was a sharp one and he'd seen something between us almost from the beginning. Because he was so sharp, I should have listened. Fawna had told me. Hell, I'd even known Aleena thought I didn't want to be seen in public with her, but I hadn't realized just how deep it had gone. Because I hadn't wanted to see.

Aleena's eyes were haunted and when I reached for her, she backed away.

"I'm not an idiot, Dominic," she said, the words hollow. She reached up to toy with her necklace and she touched the diamond collar I'd given her. She fisted her hand liked it burned to touch it and I saw her throat work. Her eyes fell away. "We don't eat together. You never once wanted to take me out. The few times I asked if we could go out, it was like I'd asked you to the Inquisition. The one time you *did* ask me something that even resembled a date, you made it quite clear what my place was."

She laughed and the sound of it stabbed through me.

"I guess I needed rules even for that. You should have explained I was expected to let perverts put their hands on me and take whatever insults rich, bitchy socialites send my way—"

The sound of shattering glass caught us both off guard. I stared at the table I'd just upended, hardly able to believe what I'd just done. It had been a long time since I'd lost control like that.

Sucking in a breath, I squeezed my eyes closed. "Stop. I...just. I fucked up. I didn't know he'd touched you. I didn't know he'd...I just didn't know. I'm sorry."

Aleena didn't say anything.

"Please don't leave me, Aleena."

Again...nothing.

Terror unlike anything I'd known in a long, long

119

time started to grow inside me and I turned, staring at her. I couldn't lose her. "I...fuck, Aleena. Just tell me what it is you want. What you need. I don't know how to do this. You want me to take you out on dates? Fine. We can do that." Desperate, I looked around. She'd dropped some clothes so I grabbed them and held them out. "Get dressed. We can go out right now. You want to go dancing? The movies? Just...just you've got to tell me how to do this because I don't know how."

"What do you mean you don't know how?" She eyed the clothes I held, almost nervously, and I realized she was still clutching clothes she'd gathered in her hands.

Feeling stupid now, I lowered my hands. I dropped down onto the bed, staring at the pale green sweater and a faded pair of jeans. "I don't...I don't do relationships, Aleena. These...they just aren't my thing. I've told you that."

"Oh, I *get* that you're not much for relationships." She toyed with the sleeve of the shirt she held, her eyes bouncing around. "Trust me, I've noticed. Because that's about all I can do. Notice. Because I can't get to know anything about you any other way."

"You..." I looked at her, then away.

Tell me about the nightmares.

I laughed sourly and surged up off the bed. I got it now. I had no doubt what had driven her to ask. Penelope had definitely pulled out all the stops tonight. I'd seen the gleam in her eyes when we'd been talking just before Eddie had pulled me aside. I knew that gleam, knew she'd been causing trouble. She knew what had happened to me. If it had happened any time recently, I doubt any amount of money could have hidden it, thanks to the wonders—or atrocities—of social media. But over a decade ago, news didn't travel the way it did now and scandals were easier to hide.

But nothing stayed hidden from everybody. Or forever.

If you had the money and knew who to ask, you could find out almost anything.

Penelope was one who had the money and she knew who to ask. I wouldn't have even put it past her to have asked my mother, though I hoped to hell that wasn't where she'd gotten her information. I'd never forgive that.

Tell me about the nightmares.

It was the last thing I wanted to do. Ever.

But it was the *only* thing I could do if I wanted to keep her. I just hoped what I told her didn't drive her away.

Swallowing hard and wishing I had something to clear away the metallic taste of my blood, I lifted my gaze and stared at Aleena.

"When I was fifteen years old, I was kidnapped."

Like it happened in slow motion, the clothes Aleena held dropped from her hands. I saw each piece. A lacy bra. A pink blouse. Jeans. A silky scrap that could only be panties. "What?" she whispered.

"I don't remember exactly how it happened—how he grabbed me. I just..." I lifted my eyes to the ceiling, trying to focus on the elegant white fan pattern instead of the memories. If I gave it like a report, I could do this. It wasn't like I hadn't talked about it a hundred times. A thousand even. "I woke up. He had me restrained. I..."

A soft gasp escaped her.

I deliberately focused on anything but her. If I looked at her, I wouldn't be able to finish this. I couldn't bear to see whatever was on her face at that moment.

"He had me for a year. I was raped. Beaten. Starved half the time. There were times when I thought I'd freeze. Other times when he'd just...go away and I'd be convinced I'd die down there, tied up and alone. Nobody even knowing what happened."

"Dominic..." Her voice broke.

Her shadow fell across my line of vision and then she touched my arm. But I had to finish this. I dropped my head, looking down at my hands.

"After about a year, I escaped. If I hadn't..." My voice trailed off for a moment, but I forced myself to go on. "They never caught him. I spent years in therapy. Tried drowning myself in alcohol and drugs and sex, but it made it worse. My life was spiraling out of control. And then, one night, right after I turned eighteen, this woman I picked up at some club...we fell asleep after and I had a nightmare. She woke me up and since the story had been in the papers, she figured out who I was."

I paused and took a deep breath, determined to finish the story. I swallowed and continued, "Instead of pitying me, she told me about her controlling ass of an ex and how she dealt with things." My hands curled into fists. "She's the one who took me to Olympus. It's a club. A bdsm club. It's where I learned that I could be in control. All the time. And it worked. I could control sex. Anger. Pain. And as long as I was in control, I couldn't...no one could..."

Aleena knelt in front of me, her hand gently cupping my chin and raising my head until we were face-to-face. My eyes were dry, but hers weren't. The tears on her face, dotting her lashes, they were for me, and they gave me the strength to say what else I needed to say.

"I don't know how to do this. I don't know how to give you what you want, but I don't want to lose you."

She didn't say anything and something cracked inside me.

I was too late.

Serving HIM continues in Vol. 5, release June 12th.

Acknowledgement

First, we would like to thank all of our readers. Without you, our books would not exist. We truly appreciate each and every one of you.

A big "thanks" goes out to all the Facebook fans, street team, beta readers, and advanced reviewers. You are a HUGE part of the success of the series.

We have to thank our PA, Shannon Hunt. Without you our lives would be a complete and utter mess. Also a big thank you goes out to our editor Lynette and our wonderful cover designer, Sinisa. You make our ideas and writing look so good.

About The Authors

MS Parker

M. S. Parker is a USA Today Bestselling author and the author of the Erotic Romance series, Club Privè and Chasing Perfection.

Living in Southern California, she enjoys sitting by the pool with her laptop writing on her next spicy romance.

Growing up all she wanted to be was a dancer, actor or author. So far only the latter has come true but M. S. Parker hasn't retired her dancing shoes just yet. She is still waiting for the call for her to appear on Dancing With The Stars.

When M. S. isn't writing, she can usually be found reading– oops, scratch that! She is always writing.

Cassie Wild

Cassie Wild loves romance. Every since she was eight years old she's been reading every romance novel she could get her hands on, always dreaming of writing her own romance novels.

When MS Parker approached her about co-authoring the Serving HIM series, it didn't take Cassie many seconds to say a big yes!!

Serving HIM is only the beginning to the collaboration between MS Parker and Cassie Wild. Another series is already in the planning stages.

Made in the USA
Monee, IL
29 March 2022

93767089R00075